Called Right

A SPICY NOVELLA

RHIANNA BURWELL

Chapter 1

Reid

The room is busy with commotion, and I try to settle into my seat, not allowing the feelings of jealousy to even phase me. If I'm being honest though, I'm doing a shitty job. I'm happy for Finn. Of course I am. He deserves this more than anyone else I know, but Jesus Christ, I'm ready for what he has. I'm ready for the love and the peace that comes with having your person with you. Feels like I've been ready for a while, but the universe likes to play tricks like that, get you ready for something and then keep it from you, make you start to sweat.

I push the thought away, trying to get over myself and stop being so self-involved. The reception hall is set up beautifully, the quartet in front playing classical music, the rows of seats full of people mingling around. The room is fancy yet simple, like they thought of everything.

I glance around the room, looking for anyone I know. I am not necessarily comfortable sitting here by myself. I am not used to feeling so out of place. It feels like I knew Finn in a past life, before all of this, before fame and money. I knew him when we were kids, and it grew from there. I saw him at his worst: when he got rejected by Cindy Warren, when he asked her to prom, when he crashed his first car with me in the passenger seat, and when he showed up drunk to meet his first girlfriend's parents. Who do you think gave him the booze? We have been ride or die since the beginning, and I wouldn't have missed this day for the world. We've kept in touch, not as much as we'd like, but we always get back together, and it feels like no time has passed. Usually, though, if we meet up with people, it's other buddies from high school, all of us catching up. But here, I feel like the only one from his past. Everyone seems to know one another, and I don't have a way in, not without Finn. So I just sit here, waiting for the wedding to start, pushing down every ounce of longing that is filling my blood and thickening in my throat.

The music changes, and suddenly, all the guests are finding their seats, and the ceremony will soon be starting. It takes a few minutes before everyone is settled, and when I shift to look behind me, Finn is walking down, glancing between the aisles, saying 'hi' to everyone. He makes eye contact with me, giving me a small head nod, and I smile back. He looks a little nervous, more nervous than I've ever seen him. Finn isn't one to get phased, but when it comes to Emma, he can't help himself.

I watch him take his place at the altar, looking at his shoes as he makes sure he is in the right spot. He then looks up as the bridal party starts to make their way down in couples. All the women wear the same color dress, a dark green, a forest green, darkening the room, giving the whiteness surrounding us life. Each dress is a different shape though, giving them all a unique flare. The men all match, their black tuxedos all exactly the same, and it looks put together, nice. They walk slowly, looking around the room and smiling, couples coming one after another until there are five people standing up at the altar with the officiant.

One last couple comes out right before the bride is going to make her entrance, and I assume it must be the best man and maid of honor, but the second I see them, my brain fucking short circuits. The maid of honor is beautiful. Her hair is up, with a few pieces falling around her shoulders, wisping against her shoulders. She smiles, and my eyes become entranced by her mouth and the way it lights up the room. She has her arm linked with the best man, but I don't look at him. She takes all of my attention as she walks down the aisle, smiling at the guests, her walk confident, her eyes bright.

She takes her place near the altar, looking out, waiting for Emma, but I just stare at her, mesmerized. The music again shifts, signaling the approach of the bride. Reluctantly, I turn away from the unknown woman and try to be present.

Chapter 2

Avery

I dry my eyes with the tissue, now crumbled and wet in my hand, my tears soaking through the thin paper. I knew I would cry, watching my sister marry the love of her life, but I didn't know I would be a fountain.

The ceremony is short. Finn and Emma both want a moment to themselves before being announced as husband and wife. Emma and I discussed this heavily, trying to figure out how much she wanted in public and how much she wanted to be by themselves. There was, and is, always a risk of the wedding getting leaked. Someone could send a video and make some easy money. The whole ceremony could be on the internet before they have even put the chairs away. They had to be careful how much was in front of people and consider how much was kept private for just the two of them. I think it's romantic, all things considered.

They both say, 'I do', and I try to will my tears away, but it is useless. I'm so happy for her that it is disgusting. We all knew it was coming. The second she brought Finn around, introducing him to our family, we knew he was the one. We knew, just based on how they looked at each other, how Finn watched her and acted as if she hung the moon. He couldn't get enough of her from the very beginning. Even now, standing there marrying her, he looks at her the same way, as if he has never wanted anyone else since he saw her for the first time, as if he couldn't imagine himself with anyone else.

She has exactly what she's always wanted: a partner who is an actual partner, a person who is there for her as much as she is there for him. She is living the dream, finding someone she can call her equal. Most of us just wish for a good hookup every now and again, desperate for, at minimum, some good sex. But for many, myself included, we don't even get that lucky.

Speaking of, it's probably a bad idea to use my sister's wedding to try to hook up with someone, right? Part of me thinks maybe. I shouldn't be using her day as a time for me to get laid, but also, I don't think I've been in a room with this many single men in a few years... probably since the last wedding I went to.

If I want to find someone to fuck, today is the day, and trust me when I say, I do.

I stopped dating a while ago, throwing in the towel after my last boyfriend gave me nothing. He wasn't bad or inattentive. I just realized that I was losing so much more than I was gaining. That's how relationships feel for me now, like something that is going to suck resources from me instead of filling me with more. It just seemed so taxing to keep dating, to keep looking for someone to be my partner, when I could just be my own partner. When I could fill my own well. I can do everything I need, can treat myself the way I've been begging men to, and now a relationship just feels like something I don't want anymore.

Ever since then, I just fuck guys. I have sex with them and leave while the night is still young, while I can still go home and take care of myself like a man never would. I have gotten so good at treating myself the way I deserve that it has started to feel like all men are good for is a quick fuck, at least in my life.

And sometimes, they can't even get that right.

But today, I have at least the smallest amount of hope. I feel like I have a real chance of getting fucked the way I deserve. If I could even get a single orgasm, from a man and not my vibrator, I think I would be happy. I'm not greedy. I'm willing to take what I can get.

Finn and Emma finally turn to the crowd, the ceremony over, and I bring myself back to the moment, trying to stop focusing on myself and my growing sexual frustration. They kiss, Finn dipping Emma, and when they come back up for air with the biggest smiles on both of their faces, they walk down the aisle. Finn's hand rests on Emma's back, as if he can't get enough of her, as if he doesn't want a moment without her, and I feel myself melt, my happiness for her overwhelming.

They exit, and the crowd makes their way into the ballroom, where the rest of the party is going to be taking place. I follow the crowd, working slowly into the space that Emma has been stressing over for the last month, discussing every detail with me. They went all out, money not being something that stopped them since Finn has plenty to go around. The room is gorgeous, with tables lining the walls, the entire room a big circle, the center of the room being a huge dance floor. The DJ is set up at the edge. He messes with his equipment, and then he takes the mic and introduces himself.

I tune him out, taking this time to glance around the room, find someone to talk to, find someone who piques my interest, find someone who could make me forget myself, even just for a moment.

My eyes catch on someone, a man, looking a little out of place, sitting at the bar, glancing around the room. I stare at him for a second, appreciating his broad shoulders in his dress shirt, his long legs, and the pants that cover them. I stare at him, for a moment longer than is probably appropriate, and as if he can feel my gaze, his head turns, our eyes connecting. I watch as he looks me over, his eyes glancing down my body, just for a moment, and they hold heat, enough heat to make my skin burn. Suddenly I see my moment, see how this night could be turned into something fucking blissful. I take a step toward him, intent on finding out if this man is the man I'm going to fuck tonight.

Chapter 3

Reid

She is goddamn gorgeous, and I can feel her eyes on me, even after I turn away. I try not to make it obvious, my attraction toward her, but I'm sure I do a crappy job, all of my emotions always being too obvious on my face.

I didn't come here to get laid. I came here to see my buddy get married. I shouldn't be focused on this. I shouldn't be worried if this woman is attracted to me too, if she is single, if she would go find a hotel room with me. I need to stop thinking with my cock, even though it is hardening in my dress pants at the mere idea of bringing her into a hotel room and bending her over the bed, desperate for both of us to be quick so no one notices we are gone.

But of course, as I push those thoughts away, telling myself that it is all a fantasy, that it probably won't even happen in my wildest dreams. I feel the movement of someone beside me, and when I spare a glance, of course, it's her. Her presence gives my fantasies a false sense of hope. I listen to her order a drink from the bartender. Her voice is light, too fucking sexy to be this close to me. She is a temptation just waiting to happen. If I was smart, I would walk away, but I'm not. I keep my ass right where it is, enjoying being close to her a little too much.

I glance over at her, her dark hair in a pretty hairstyle on her head, a few stray pieces sneaking out, framing her face. My eyes connect with hers, just for a second, before she looks away, glancing around the room as if she wasn't checking me out.

Holy shit.

I think I just caught her checking me out.

I feel my stomach somersault, and my nerves are shot. How do I even start a conversation? I'm not used to dating, not like this. I live in a small town, and most people know each other. This makes conversation easy. Of course, I still go out and pick women up for a quick hookup. But here, there's this pressure. I know she is the maid of honor. I know she is connected to Finn in a big way. If I make an ass of myself, he will hear about it.

I search my brain. I am desperate for something to say. I desperately want to start a conversation, but my mouth goes dry. Words aren't able to form even if I had them. The bartender sets her drink next to her, and she thanks him, standing up from her seat. She gives me a quick glance with her eyebrows raised and a challenging look in her eyes. She turns, intent on walking away.

"You know Finn?" I blurt out without thinking. I didn't know what else to say. I panicked. I feel my cheeks redden, just barely, as I wait for her to answer. I know this is what I was worried about. Here I am, making a fool out of myself. I can't even be mad at myself, though, because I see her give me a soft smile. She walks back to her seat and positions her body close to mine.

"Emma, actually," she replies, her voice amused. I smile back. I am such an idiot, but at the very least, I'm an idiot with her attention. So, I think I can call that a win.

"Let me guess," I say as I look her up and down. I love the excuse to check her out without suspicion. "Her sister?" I ask, seeing similar small details between the two: the shape of their faces, the way they look when they smile, but their hair color is completely different. While Emma is a fiery redhead, the woman in front of me has dark brown hair, making her entire complexion look warm.

"You got it. Although to be fair, people have asked if we are twins before," she says with a smirk. Her smirk really shouldn't make my pants tight, but it does.

"Avery, right?" I ask. My brain is finally working, and I remember Finn talking about Emma's sister a few times.

"You've heard about me?" she asks, a twinkle in her eyes. She is so fucking pretty it isn't even funny. Plus, the look in her eyes makes her look fucking sexier than I care to admit.

"Only good things," I say with a smile. I hope I am coming off flirtatiously. I want to bring my A-game for the woman in front of me. I want to impress her–probably more than I should. I should probably walk away and leave her alone. Yet, as long as she is humoring me... as long as she is paying attention to me... I can't bring myself to leave.

"Okay, my turn," she says, her eyes trailing my body, making my cock jump at her attention. She doesn't give any hint as to if she sees the bulge in my pants, but part of me hopes she does. My skin feels hot under her gaze. She does one more sweep up and down, lighting my body on fucking fire. I should not have come here so horny. I don't know how I'm supposed to hold myself back when I have someone like her sitting in front of me, mischief in her gaze.

"Take your time," I say, my voice light, full of humor as her eyes sweep over my body, not missing an inch.

"Shut up," she replies, her eyes darting to mine, her cheeks staining pink. "I was just doing thorough research," she says matter-of-factly. My confidence rises as I realize that I don't believe her. I nod at her, my eyebrows raised, as if she is full of shit, and we both know she is. "Anyway, I'm going with... friend?" she says, a question in her voice.

"What? You don't think I could pass as his brother?" I say, my hand coming to my chest as I feign hurt. She laughs at me, instantly rolling her eyes.

"I figured if you were his brother, I would've met you before. Plus, you weren't at the family table, Einstein," she says, her logic sound and her confidence extremely sexy.

"Maybe we are estranged. I'm the brother he is super jealous of," I reply, pausing for dramatic effect. "He would never admit that, though." Avery throws her head back laughing, which makes me smile. She looks at me with adoration and humor, and I feel myself swell with pride. I am enjoying the way I feel under her gaze.

"And what is he jealous of exactly?" she asks, her head cocking to the side, egging me on. I shouldn't like how she smiles at me with challenge and encouragement glinting in her eyes. I shouldn't like how it makes me want to do whatever she says. I feel desperate to get her approval. I shouldn't even be talking to someone I know that I have zero chance with, but here I am. I will soak up her attention as long as she'll give it to me.

"C'mon, give me some amount of credit here. My good looks, obviously," I say, once again pretending like she is hurting my ego. She laughs again, raising her eyebrows like I'm full of shit.

"Because he isn't good-looking, right?" Her voice is light, filled with honey. She looks at me like I hung the moon, and my jokes are the only thing getting her through the night. God, I want it to be true. I want to bask in that look for as long as humanly possible.

This honestly doesn't happen to me, not like this. I've never been interested in someone like this. I never hit it off with somebody right off the bat. Usually, the women I'm interested in passes right by me on their way to Finn. I guess it helps that her sister is married to him, but still, it feels surreal to have the full attention of someone so attractive, especially because she knows how amazing she looks in that fucking dress tonight.

Yet, here she is. She is still sitting right there, giving me all of her attention.

"You mean that troll over there?" I ask, throwing my thumb over my shoulder, and pointing to one of my longest friends. I know that he is the best-looking guy in the room. She rolls her eyes again. The smile on her face captivates me. She pretends to consider for a second, and then she nods as if she sees my point.

"You're just a little cocky, huh?" she asks, her words going right to my fucking pants. I have to force myself to hold back a groan. It is insane the things she is doing to my body, even from the chair over. She isn't even touching me. I lean closer to her. I need to close some of the distance. I need her to invade all of my senses. My knee bumps hers, her heat radiating around me. My entire body is tuned into her. I feel my cock stiffening, aching in my pants. The stupid thing is making it hard to concentrate on anything other than her lips and how amazing they would look wrapped around my cock while I beg for more.

"Say that again," I whisper. My voice is almost nonexistent, but I know she hears me. I watch her body respond to me, too. Her spine stiffens. Her lips part, and I soak it in, loving every subtle shift. I don't think. I don't question my actions. I feel like I'm moving on instinct, desperate to hear that singular word from her mouth again.

She looks me over with a smile on her face. She knows exactly what she is doing to me. She knows exactly what kind of effect she is having on me and probably loves it, if the smile on her face tells me anything.

"Cock-y," she whispers with a smile, separating the word into two. She stares at me with fucking sex eyes. Her tongue peeks out, wetting her bottom lip before she bites it, looking at me with sin in her eyes, and God, do I want to indulge. I hold back a groan, desperate to hear the word from her mouth again, thinking of a million different positions I want her to say that in, thinking of all the ways she could use her mouth against me.

"Jesus Christ," I mutter under my breath, our bodies moving closer to each other. Her mouth is only a few inches from mine, and I want to break the distance more than anything. I want her lips on mine, her lipstick smudged against my skin. I want her body pressed against mine, her tits pressed against my chest, and her legs wrapped around me. I want to show her all the ways I can use this cock-y "attitude" I've got, but of course, of fucking course, my eyes snag on the clock directly behind her. I see the time, and I realize I'm already late.

"I-I... Fuck," I mutter, turning away from her. I down my drink, not even remembering when it was placed in front of me, turning it into more of a shot than anything. "Fuck, I'm sorry, I gotta go," I mutter, frustrated with myself. I knew scheduling my flight so early was a bad idea, but it was the only flight back home that was available within the next four days, and I have a hundred work meetings on Monday that I can't miss. Being a CFO is great until moments like this when I'm leaving behind my fucking dream woman at a bar.

"You're leaving?" she asks, her eyes following my sudden movements, her eyes wide. I soak her in for another second, kicking myself for not indulging in a little vacation. Finn even offered. He ended up renting everyone hotel rooms for the week so he could hang out with everyone before he goes on his honeymoon with Emma, both of them flying across the country for a few months. I wish I could have just let myself stay. I already know a hundred ways I could use the extra time, most of them with both me and Avery naked, but I know I need to leave. I don't have time to indulge in something as delicious as her right now.

"I have a flight I have to catch. I have to be back at the office on Monday, and if I miss this fucking flight, I'm going to be ruined. I'm sorry," I mutter, looking at her desperately. I need her to understand. I feel like a complete bastard and I know it is for good reason. I can't believe I'm walking away from this right now.

"No, it's fine. I should probably get back to the dance floor anyway before Emma comes looking for me," she says with a small smile, her disappointment leaking through, just barely, just enough to make me kick myself mentally one more time.

"Let me give you my number," I offer as I rise from my chair. I know that I needed to leave about five minutes ago if I were to have any chance to make this flight, but there is no way I'm going to leave this beautiful woman without giving her some way to contact me. I need some way to make this a little better.

"Oh... yeah, sure," she says, her voice weak, unconvinced.

"You don't want it?" I ask frantically, desperate for her to take it. I suddenly wonder if I misread this entire situation.

"No, no, it's not that. It's just... we probably don't even live close enough to each other for it to matter," she says with a shrug of her shoulders, but I'm not convinced. I did not just flirt my ass off with the person I have been staring at since I first saw her to get fucked over by this goddamn flight.

"Please?" I ask, knowing I probably sound pathetic but not caring for a fucking second. "It'll make me feel better about leaving so suddenly," I say, going for pity if nothing else. We might never see each other again, but I don't want to leave this without at least trying to give my best.

I watch her eyes soften, and I know what she is going to say before she even opens her mouth. "Okay, fine," she says, "But I'm not promising to use it," she warns, but I don't think about that. I just need to know I tried to get this gorgeous woman to take my number, to give me the tiniest chance.

"That's fine," I say. I feel like I won, even though the odds are that she isn't going to call or want to talk to some random guy she met at her sister's wedding. I grab the nearest napkin, ask the bartender for a pen, and quickly scribble my name and number on the thin piece of paper. I hand it to her with a small smile, her face full of curiosity, interest, and just the hint of disappointment. I turn away before I get any more ideas, like ditching work to stay with Avery even just a minute longer.

Chapter 4

Avery

He's gone before I even have a chance to reply. The only proof that our conversation actually happened is the napkin sitting in my hand with his number scrawled on it, his handwriting messy.

I stare down at the napkin, letting my disappointment sink into my gut, instantly ridiculing myself for even feeling this way. It's honestly so fucking stupid. I just met this man. I shouldn't be disappointed that he has to leave.

But in the back of my head, in the way way back, I feel the disappointment, the ideas I had for tonight, of all the things I wanted us to do, fading away. He looked at me with so much lust, so much sex in his gaze. He would've been such a good lay, and it has been way too long for me. I am pissed I didn't get a chance to fuck him, for him to use his body against mine, to pull noises from me, to fuck me good and hard, but now I'm coming to terms with the fact that it isn't going to happen, no matter how turned on I am, how desperate I am.

Emma and Finn are paying for hotel rooms for everyone for the week, giving us all a luxury vacation after their wedding. I just assumed everyone was staying, not wanting to give up the chance to miss out on a free vacation like me, but I must have been mistaken, because the only man I wanted to sleep with left in the middle of the after party.

Emma told me that she was flying people in from all over the country. I guess Finn didn't grow up in the city, so most of his childhood friends are pretty far away from him. Based on what I know about this guy, I doubt we live in the same time zone anyway, so having his number doesn't mean shit. We had one chance to fuck, and we lost it.

I push my disappointment down, still feeling like an idiot for even feeling disappointment in the first place, and I order another drink. I stuff the napkin in my purse while I wait for my drink, not wanting to look at it anymore, not liking the reminder that I'm going to my room alone tonight unless I find someone else who piques my interest like he did, which is unlikely.

I shoot my drink back the second it touches down at the bar, desperate to bring myself back to the moment. I drag myself back to the dance floor, doing my best to convince myself to forget the entire conversation even happened in the first place. It was probably stupid for me to think it was going to go beyond the bar. I just liked the image of him in my hotel room, half his body under the covers, his bare chest exposed to me, his eyes on me and allowing them to consume me.

I feel my skin flush at the thought of his body at my disposal. I think about all the things I want to do to him, all the places I want to lick, desperate just for a taste, but I push the thoughts away instantly, feeling foolish for even going that far with my imagination.

I dance with Emma for most of the night, intent on forgetting that interaction ever even happened. The party ends, and Finn and Emma say goodnight, heading to their hotel room with promises to see us all tomorrow. I thank them for flying me out and paying for me to have a mini beach vacation with them, too. I am overly grateful for their generosity.

Everyone starts to filter out of the party quickly, heading to their hotel rooms, and I do the same, desperate to sleep off all of the booze I consumed and finally rest my feet. I've been awake since early this morning, in the bride suite tending to

Emma's every desire, and although I loved every minute of it, it was fucking exhausting.

I crash hard, falling into bed before I've even had a chance to wash my face, but I don't care. I'm too tired to give a shit. I'll deal with the consequences tomorrow.

Chapter 5

Avery

I wake up the next morning unable to think because of how hard my head is fucking pounding. Overall, the hangover isn't awful. Just a nasty headache that makes me want to stay in bed all day, but I've been here enough to know that I'll feel better after a bottle of water and some food, so I force myself to get up, desperate for anything that will relieve the pounding taking place in my skull.

I force myself to open the curtains, the sun blinding me instantly, making my headache that much worse. I grab a bottle of water from the mini-fridge in the room, not even allowing myself to look at the price, knowing it will be insane, and grab some meds from my purse, desperate for some kind of relief. I take them quickly, my eyes catching on the napkin poking out of my purse, my mind flooding with memories instantly, making my stomach churn. The flirting, the touching, the sexual energy, the whispering in my goddamn ear, the way he made my entire body feel fucking alive, and then, the sudden departure, leaving me unsatisfied in all the worst ways.

It is easier to dismiss everything that I felt last night when the light of day is gleaming in, sobering me up. I was probably imagining the connection, the booze soaking into my bones, making everyone seem more attractive, more attentive. I was looking for someone at the wedding, and I found someone who checked a couple of boxes, but that doesn't have to mean anything. I do my best to convince myself I didn't miss out on much, that he wouldn't have been that good in bed anyway. I do my best to push him out of my mind, desperate to stop thinking about what could have been and start enjoying the week-long vacation that Finn and Emma have set me up with.

I put on a pair of sandals and a typical outfit for me: a pair of cotton shorts and a strappy tank top, making me feel comfortable and cute at the same time.

I make my way down to the lobby, checking several times that I have my key, knowing that my brain isn't operating fully, and I would rather save myself the embarrassment of dragging myself to the front desk to get a new one.

"You look like shit," a familiar voice says next to me, humor in her tone. I turn to the side, making eye contact with my newlywed sister. Emma looks like she just woke up from a perfect night's sleep, her entire body radiating energy and youth, her red hair silky and curled, and her skin glowing. I feel happiness swell in my belly, loving watching my sister thrive, loving seeing her at her best.

She has always been pretty, her red hair a beautiful contrast to her light skin, her dark eyes bringing her entire look together, but since she met Finn, she has looked happy. She walks through the world like it was made for her, and maybe it was. It gave her exactly what she wanted and then gave her a little more, and I honestly couldn't be happier for her. She deserves it.

"Don't tell me you slept all night. That would be a pretty crappy wedding night," I mutter, looking at her with a smirk while we walk through the lobby side by side as I try to find the breakfast area, insistent on finding a cup of coffee and something to soak up the booze from last night. She smiles at me mischievously, and I know I'm about to get a little too much information about their wedding night. Talking about her sex life isn't weird for us, at least not anymore. When we were younger, neither of us wanted to know about it. It was a don't-ask-don't-tell situation, but as we got older, she became less of my sister and more of my friend, and naturally, we just started telling each other everything. But still, I have to look the man in the eye. It was easier when she was telling me about meaningless hookups. Now I see Finn at Christmas dinner and have to try to forget all of the nasty things Emma has told me.

"You'd sleep pretty good too, after three orgasms," she mutters, sending me a wink. I pretend to shudder as if grossed out. She rolls her eyes and I smile back, silently communicating with her in a way that makes me feel particularly close to her.

"What are you up to today, Mrs. Declan?" I ask, glancing out the windows of the lobby, wincing at the bright light but also yearning to feel the sun on my skin, to tan and soak up all of its rays, letting them heal me from the outside in–after I get rid of this goddamn headache, of course, when the light is a little less blinding.

"Oh my god, don't say that. He is still trying to convince me to take his last name, and if he hears you say that he is never going to shut up about it," she mutters, looking around, checking to see if Finn is nearby. I just smile at her and shake my head, enjoying how possessive Emma's new husband is of her. He knows it is old school for her to take his last name, but he just likes to hear it, likes to think of her as his just as much as he thinks of himself as hers.

"Isn't that something you should have figured out before you tied the knot?" I ask, laughing, knowing they have been going back and forth with this for ages, neither of them wanting to give in and let the other have their way. I understand it's a big decision, but they have been discussing this for months now.

"You would think. We filled out all the paperwork and kept my name the same, but he keeps trying to convince me to just change it after. It seems like too much of a hassle, but he loves the idea of me with his last name. He's acting like a caveman, and although it's kinda hot, it's annoying," she says with a smile and a roll of her eyes, her happiness so evident that I smile too, her joy infectious, even though I still feel like roadkill. "Anyway, I think we are going to the pool. I gotta at least attempt to tan since we are here," she says as we finally walk into the breakfast area, the smell of pastries filling the air, my stomach grumbling the second it hits my nose.

The hotel is nice, nice enough to wow me. The entire thing is complimentary, meaning every meal is free and served buffet style. I figured it wouldn't be anything special, but I couldn't be more wrong. There are about a hundred stations to pick from. Fresh fruit and warm pastries and coffees with a hundred creams line the walls, and tables fill the rest of the room, half of them occupied by people getting as much as they can.

"Wanna meet at the pool once you are done eating?" Emma asks as she looks at what I can only assume is my ravenous face, my hunger finally hitting me, my body desperate for some nutrients after I drowned in enough alcohol to last a lifetime.

"Yeah, that's perfect," I mutter, barely paying attention to her anymore. I make my way over to almost every station, at least looking around, wanting to familiarize myself with the choices since we have another week here, and I'm going to make sure they get their money's worth. It's the least I could do.

I fill a plate full of food, pour a steaming cup of coffee, and have one of the best breakfasts of my life, finally feeling like a person afterward.

Chapter 6

Avery

I'm drunk for the second day in a row, something I haven't done since college. Me and Emma are sitting under the sun, the sun that is going down now, but we have been here all fucking day, soaking in the sun, putting on layer after layer of SPF, desperate not to burn. We are drinking fruity complimentary drinks and gossiping about literally everything, soaking in every second together, because after this she will be gone for a while, traveling around the world, living her best life. I can't help but admit that I'm going to fucking miss her, the alcohol making me feel sappier than I have in a long time.

It has been nice just to be around her again. We see each other often. We Facetime each other every other day, but it is nice to just be around her for uninterrupted hours again, like when we were teenagers and lived together, but now we aren't bitches to each other.

"Okay, I need to go find my husband. Let's hope he didn't find his way to bingo night. He takes his gambling a little too seriously sometimes," Emma mutters, finally getting up from her lounger and grabbing her drink and towel off the table. I, honestly, can't imagine Finn playing bingo. The thought of it causes giggles to bubble out of me, and suddenly, I realize how drunk I am, the alcohol making everything seem a little *too* funny. I raise myself into a sitting position, my head instantly feeling light, the booze hitting me a little harder than I first thought. "Goodnight. See you tomorrow," she yells behind her, already walking away from me.

The sun is low in the sky, hinting at the sunset, but I'm already exhausted. The sun, the booze, and the swimming we did earlier have worn me out. I stand up from my lounger, giving myself a second to find my balance before I start gathering my things. It is easier to drink a few too many when you are sitting down when you can't tell how fucking dizzy you are. It isn't until you're standing that you realize those lemon drops were probably a bad idea, but when they are free, it's so goddamn hard to say no.

I grab the rest of my stuff, intent on going back to my room and maybe tucking into bed and watching TV, having a round with my vibrator, and then sleeping for twelve hours straight. Even just the sound of that makes my body hum, desperate for a quiet night in, and, for once in my life, relax.

I haven't taken a vacation for so long, probably too long. I'm dedicated to work, and I always have been, and that makes it hard to find time off. Add that to the fact that I'm in digital marketing, a field that never seems to rest, and I haven't had a relaxing week in years.

It probably takes me longer than it should to find my room, the numbers blurring in my vision, but I finally make it back, finally finding the correct room. The warm feeling that was covering my body from all the booze and the sun seems to evaporate in the silent and empty room. It suddenly feels a little too quiet, a little too empty, and I feel my stomach churn as the door clicks behind me. I walk over to the bed, stumbling into a sitting position, my body swaying as the alcohol moves through me, and I try to keep myself steady, but it doesn't work well.

I've been single for a while, and I've gotten used to being alone. I've come to enjoy it, enjoying my own company more than I would keeping company with most other people, but every now and again, the loneliness will hit me hard, making me wish I had someone to be with me when I want it, instead of alone just being my default. I don't wish for it often, but I do in moments like this when I wish someone was here to take care of me, to smile at me while I almost fall over, just happy to be around me, just happy to have me in his arms. I want the comfort and stability of a relationship, but anytime I think about going out and finding the real thing or think about putting in that effort, it makes me want to throw up. I like the idea of it, though.

I do like the fantasy. Especially when I'm drunk and horny as hell. I wish I had someone to take care of me in a whole different kind of way.

My eyes dart to my purse, the napkin the stranger left for me, his number scrawled on it, sitting right at the top, calling to me. I stare at it for just a second, considering. I know it's stupid. Nothing is going to come from it, so using his number is a total waste of time for both of us in the long run, but instead of listening to the rational voice inside of me, I walk toward my purse. I scoop the napkin out and unfold it, reading the number in front of me, debating with myself, my drunk voice telling me one thing while my rational voice tells me something completely different.

I plop on the bed, weighing my options, both sides of myself fighting against what to do. I stare at the napkin, and the numbers blur together, my mind feeling fuzzy, my body feeling keyed up, a little too intrigued at the idea of calling him, a little too tempted.

My drunk brain keeps whispering about how it doesn't need to mean anything, that even if it doesn't go anywhere, we could use each other for a good time. I'm not looking for a boyfriend right now. I'm looking for some goddamn relief, someone to have fun with. That's what he was supposed to be last night, but he had a plane to catch. What is wrong with still having fun with him with no other expectations? What's wrong with having a little help while I use my vibrator? What's wrong with both of us finding relief in each other?

Nothing. Nothing is wrong with that.

We don't have to be with each other to use each other, to get better orgasms out of the night. Sexting and phone sex aren't as good as the real thing. Everyone can admit that, but it would be better than solo, better than doing it all myself.

I type the number into my phone with that thought in my brain, my body already coming alive at the idea, at the possibility. The booze running through me makes my skin warm, makes me feel light and breezy, carefree. It makes me feel like I can do this: message him and ask for all the things I want. Ask him to take care of this fucking ache between my legs and beg him to make me feel good, make me forget that I'm alone in this hotel room...about to fall asleep by myself.

I'm horny, and I'm drunk, and I want someone to take care of me, make me cum before I fall to sleep, and I need it to be him, not some stranger down at the bar, because as much as I don't want to admit it, he's been on my mind. My body remembers him, remembers how desperately I wanted him to take me upstairs. It's like an itch that I can't scratch, and now I'm determined to take care of it, right now.

My fingers hover over the message box for a moment, not knowing what I want to say or how I want to get this started. My drunk brain misfires, nothing coming to me, everything sounding stupid. I sit there for a few seconds, my mind feeling blank, feeling a little stupid for putting this much thought into my message to this stranger who I don't even really know, when I finally say fuck it, and type the first thing that comes to mind, not caring how it sounds, not caring if it is too bold, my brain feeling too horny to think, to care.

Well, maybe I care a little, but I continue to tell myself I don't, hitting send before I can second-guess myself anymore.

If you would have come up to my room, what would you have done?

I read the message back to myself, feeling bold, feeling empowered, and a little bit nervous. I don't know what time it is for him, so I don't know if he's even gonna respond. This may have been a stupid idea, but the second I start to doubt myself, I see the three dots, indicating that he is typing out a response, and I let my body relax on my bed, desperate for some kind of release, a release that only he can give me.

Chapter 7

Reid

I stare at the message in front of me. My cock hardens at the mere thought of what I wanted to do that night. I've been waiting to hear from her. I've been desperate for her to want this as badly as I do. I am desperate to finish what we started, and I had started to lose hope that she would use my number, but the text stares back at me, confirming that maybe we are in this crazy attraction together.

For the hundredth time, I curse at myself for needing to work on Monday, for not giving myself the vacation I deserved. I could have been with her, could have gotten her out of my system, but now I'm just desperate for her, for that release we never got a chance to chase. It burns into my skin, making me horny and uncomfortable, making me fidgety.

I lay back in my bed, knowing I should go to sleep, knowing I need to be awake early in the morning, but not caring. My heart pounds as I start to type out my reply, my gut already knowing where this is headed, already knowing what is going to happen tonight, and the anticipation is like a fucking drug.

There were a lot of things I wanted to do to you, still do actually.

I hit send quickly, not wanting to second guess my reply, but when I see it is delivered, I read it again, wincing at how lame it sounds. I don't do this. That is, stuff over the phone. Flirting and sexting from hundreds of miles away. I have had sex with my fair share of women, but truthfully, this isn't something I'm experienced in. And, part of that, makes me nervous. My phone pings with a reply, and my eyes dart down. I read it instantly, not even having bothered to exit the text thread.

Like what?

I sit there, my fingers hovering over my phone, my hair a fucking mess from the long day I've had. My body is naked, my cock hard, but my mind stutters. I don't know how to start this. I know what she wants. I know what we both want, but I'm not sure how to get us there. My fingers move aimlessly, my mind whirling. My nerves start to invade my senses as I push myself to think. Once again, I type something quickly, not second-guessing it. I then wince at it after it is delivered. I hate how bad I am at this.

Like kiss you

I stare at the screen, waiting and waiting and waiting for her to reply. The message is instantly read, but she doesn't start typing right away. I feel my anxiety creep up my spine. My mind begins running away with it, convincing me that I've already messed this up. I've screwed up, something that hasn't even started. Ugh. We haven't even had a chance to explore whatever this is. If I've already messed this up, it would be no one's fault but my own.

My phone buzzes in front of me and makes me jump. When I glance at it, my body instinctively expects a text. I see a random number calling me. It is the same random number I was just texting with. I hit the answer button before I have a second to think. My hands are just moving on autopilot as my brain stutters to keep up.

"Hello?" I ask hesitantly, not knowing what to expect.

"Hey," she replies, her voice light, sexy over the phone.

"What's up?" I ask, my brain blank, in straight panic mode. I've never felt this out of my element, this lost when it comes to women, and it's throwing me off of my game. I'm not usually this bad, this clumsy, this unsure of myself. I feel like I need to smack myself and get myself back on track. I don't dare pull the phone away from my ear. My body glued to her voice instantly. I just didn't expect her to call, to be on the phone speaking with me all of a sudden, and I don't know how to act.

"That's what you consider dirty talk?" she asks, her voice light, mocking me in a playful way, a way that makes me smile lightly, remembering exactly why I liked her at the wedding, remembering how we clicked so well.

"I–uh," I pause, feeling a little more comfortable but still not knowing what to say. I laugh lightly at myself as awkwardness fills me. I'm not used to having someone so straightforward talking to me, someone so willing to clear the air.

"Usually, when I'm trying to impress a woman, I have her in my bed," I say awkwardly, my mind instantly filling with images of her in my bed, my body responding to the thought.

"Too bad you had a plane to catch," she says, and I can imagine the way her eyebrows rise in challenge, giving me shit.

"Trust me, I've been kicking myself since I left," I reply and she laughs, the sound making me smile. The sound of her laugh calms my anxiety.

"As you should be," she says boldly, but her words slur, just barely, and it makes me pause.

"Are you drunk?" I ask, sitting up a little straighter in my bed. My comforter falls down as I do, exposing me to the cold air of my bedroom.

"Maybe," she whispers, her voice so fucking sweet it hurts.

"Is that the only reason you called?" I ask, trying not to sound deflated. "Because you're drunk?"

"No," she answers, putting me at ease. "It helped give me the courage to text, but I've been thinking about you all day, wishing you were here to finish what we started," she murmurs. Her voice is like velvet through the phone, and I feel myself react. My cock hardens. It aches in my boxers. It begs to be touched.

"Well, I'm glad you called," I reply. I give her just a hint of myself. I give just a tiny bit of vulnerability to this woman who has been on my mind all day, too.

"Are you?" she says flirtatiously, a smile in her voice, and I smile too.

"Yeah, part of me wondered if I'd ever hear from you," I admit.

"I wondered the same thing," she says softly. She pauses, like she is thinking. I wait, feeling like she has more to say. "It's messy, with you being friends with Finn."

"It doesn't have to be," I reply lightly. I want to know how she is feeling. It was so easy when we were at the bar together, in another world. It seemed like nothing mattered then, like any mistake we might make would disappear when we left, but now I'm home and that illusion is shattered.

Yet, still, I don't want to get off the phone.

"That's true. I could just use you instead of porn," she says slightly with a small laugh. I feel the air fucking leave my lungs.

"I have literally never thought of anything better," I reply, my entire body tuned into this conversation. I want nothing more than to be used by her. I want her to find pleasure in me. The only problem is... I'm not used to this. How do I do this? How do I pleasure her while being miles away from her? I've never really had phone sex. I've never tried to have my voice be the thing to get women off, but honestly, I'm not going to turn down anything she is offering.

"What are you like in bed?" she asks, her voice low and relaxed. I imagine her in her hotel bed, the blankets covering her, with the phone to the side of her ear as she snuggles deeper, getting comfortable while talking to me.

I'm thankful for the slight conversation change, wanting more of a lead-in if this is where things are going. If we are going to use each other for pleasure over the phone, then I need some time to get my bearings.

I think for a moment, trying to find the right words for what I'm like in bed. "Dominant," I reply hoarsely. My cock strains against the fabric of my boxers, this entire conversation driving my blood pressure higher.

"Really? I have a dom on my hands, huh?" God, even the cadence of her voice is driving me wild. She has this way of deepening it when she says something sexy. She knows exactly how to change her pitch to make my skin burn.

"I'm known to dabble in a little bit of everything, but I would say I like to be in control," I reply, trying to push away the distracting throbbing that is happening under my boxers. I am trying to stay present in the conversation and not sink into how badly I wish she was here, with me, letting me touch her.

"I feel like I'm a little control freak too. I can never shut my brain off," she says lightly, a sigh in her voice, her annoyance with that aspect of herself expressed by her words.

"Maybe you just need someone to shut it off for you," I say, my mind whirling with all the ways I could do just that. There are so many ways I could make her forget who she is, make her pleasure completely overpower her.

"Maybe," she says, her voice a fucking purr. Her voice is so sweet that it isn't fair that she is across the country, too far away from me right now. "Do you think you could shut it off for me?" she asks, sinfully. Her intention is so fucking clear.

"You're dangerous," I admit softly, my voice a little gravelly. I can feel the pull to touch myself. I want to stroke myself to just the sound of her voice, but I hold myself back, not fully knowing if I should. Is that allowed?

"What? Are you horny or something?" she says with mock innocence. My eyes close as her words rush through me. God, she knows exactly what she has been doing to me. She understands exactly how insane she is driving me.

"I have a brat on my hands, don't I?" Where there are brats, there are punishments. We aren't there, yet. We both know that. We don't know each other well enough to even pretend to play that game, but anticipation is a powerful drug. I'm already imagining all the ways I could overcome her with pleasure and all the ways I could use her body against her.

"I–I don't really know," she admits, her voice pulled back, just barely. I wait and give her just a second to think. When her voice comes back strong and confident again, I'm glad I did. "I've never really thought about it. Usually, men just want me to do all the work. They want a blow job and want me to be on top, and they just want to sit there and enjoy it," she says, almost thoughtfully, like she is just now realizing what has been missing during sex for her. "Maybe you could help me find out," she says, her meaning so clear.

I want to so bad, but I'm not even sure where to start. I'm confident in the bedroom, used to having women falling apart around me, used to doing whatever I can to make a woman cum, but this is out of my wheelhouse, and something about that makes me nervous. Nervousness is not a feeling I'm used to having.

"About that," I mutter, clearing my throat. "I've never really had phone sex," I say softly, a small wince taking over my face while I wait for her reaction. I wait for her to make fun of me or make me feel bad for never doing something like this.

"Really?" she says, shock filling her voice. "That's surprising. You talked such a big game at the bar," she says, and I can hear her smile.

"I do have a big game, but I expected to show you in person, not from this many miles away," I admit, my face feels hot, and I know it must be reddening. I'm suddenly glad she isn't here and can't see me right now.

"Do you need me to teach you?" she says, her voice so fucking sexy, so low. God, she's good at this. "Do you need a lesson?" she asks, and I swear to God I'm gonna lose it. Having her voice on the other end of the phone is fucking torture. Not having her here is fucking torture. Not having my hands on her or my lips on her skin is fucking torture.

"Yes," I say roughly. "You can show me exactly what you like." My voice is hoarse, my cock stiff, and my blood boiling. The idea of her, teaching me, coaching me through how to do something, turns me on. But much more than that, she'd be teaching me what she likes, what turns her on—my own masterclass on Avery.

"I usually just start with all the things I want to do, what I would do if I was there with you, instead of miles away," she teases. Her voice is slow and indicates how well she knows what her words are doing to me. "Usually, I start touching myself too, working myself up," she says. Images pop up in my head of her lying on her back as she touches herself while thinking of fucking me. The thoughts overfill my brain and overload it with visuals of her.

"Are you touching yourself right now?" I ask. I need for her to be touching herself. I need the confirmation. The thought of her on the other end of this phone, with her fingers against her clit, her pussy weeping for me, makes me harder than I've been in so long. It makes me want to catch a flight and take care of this, take care of her and her growing need, but I stay still, my cock tenting the blankets. I wait for her to speak. I wait for the confirmation that I should jerk off.

"Maybe," she whispers, the tiniest fucking moan in her words. I curse under my breath, pushing the blankets away. I pull my cock out of my boxers instantly gripping it and hold back a moan myself.

"I'm gonna stroke my cock, while you tell me about the nasty things you wanted me to do, okay?" I ask. I am surprised by my sudden, forceful need for this. We have been playing back and forth for too long, and know I need this release. I wanted it to be with her in person but over the phone will have to do.

"Yes, sir," she says, the smile evident in her voice, and I feel my jaw drop. My cock is so hard. It throbs in my hand.

"You're a fucking vixen, aren't you?" I ask, exacerbated. I feel like the air was stripped from my lungs, ripped out by that one word. She shouldn't know what she just did to me, but based on her giggle across the phone, she does. She knows exactly how much she influences me. "You got me thinking you are sweet, but I think you are a siren in disguise," I say on a breath, stroking up and down. Wishing to God she was right here in front of me, saying these things in my ear, whispering all of this while we watch each other jerk off. I wish I was seeing her, watching her tits move with each breath, watching her fingers stroke herself, watching the pleasure take over her face the longer we went. God, I want it so much. Lust wraps around my spine, taking me hostage.

"I don't know what you're talking about," she says with a breath, and I wish I could see how wet she is. I wish I could hear the wet sounds coming from her pussy. She acts so innocent, but we both know it is a farce.

"Walk me through this whole phone sex thing, so I can hear you cum," I say, my voice fucking thick with arousal as I slowly stroke my cock, moving my hand up and down the shaft, my entire body tensing as I try to hold it together. Usually, I don't have a hard time keeping myself from cumming early, but listening to her on the other end of the phone, playing with herself, breathy moans leaking from her mouth, so quiet, almost like she doesn't want me to know how much this is affecting her, is driving me fucking wild. *She* is driving me fucking wild.

"I wanted you to come up to my hotel room, strip me bare, and eat me out until I was cumming all over your face," she murmurs, her voice alluring, as if she doesn't have the energy to be playful anymore, as if her body has stolen that away and replaced it with this desire. I feel it, too, and I know exactly what she is going through.

"Jesus Christ," I mutter, my hand moving faster. "I would eat you out all fucking night if you would let me," I say, wanting that, wanting to feel her against my face as she cums, her body tense against mine. I want it all, to feel her wetness, to slide my tongue in between her slick pussy, and to open her up for me alone, exposing her cunt to me.

"Fuck," she moans out. "I don't think I would be able to last long before I would beg you to fuck me though." She is driving me insane, her little sounds, the static, as if she is wiggling around, unable to stay still while she touches herself. "Even now, my pussy is fucking aching to be filled."

"Fuck, you are doing so fucking good," I moan out, my cock so hard in my hand. It is so hard against my strokes, and I want nothing more than to cum, to show her how much this is influencing me, to show her how keyed up my body is, something I didn't think she could do from so far away, but I hold off, needing to hear her cum first, needing to hear how loud she gets when she is finally close. "Tell me what you are doing right now. Tell me how good it feels," I say, then add, "Please," I rush out, needing to know, needing a visual to add to the sounds running through my phone.

"I'm playing with my pussy, my fingers stroking back and forth over my clit. My back keeps fucking arching because it feels so good," she moans, and I feel my orgasm start, my entire body tuned into her words, but I slow down, needing to hear this, needing to stay present with her. "I'm so fucking wet, I'm drenching my fucking fingers," she says, and I imagine it all, her wetness running down to her ass as it drips out of her.

"Fuck, I wish I was there," I mutter between clenched teeth as I try to last. "Baby, I'm gonna cum soon. There is no way I'm gonna last much longer with you like this," I say, my voice a plea, desperate for her to be there with me, to tell me that she is close too, that I'm not going through this intense feeling alone.

"I'm close too," she moans, her voice making my entire body tingle, every nerve ending standing up, come alive.

"Fuck, I need to hear you cum," I groan out, demanding. I need this. I need this more than I need to breathe. My entire mind is swept up in this moment, in this orgasm, in the sound of her voice through my phone. I can think of nothing else. I can focus on nothing other than her. I need to hear her finish. I need to hear her orgasm take her because I'm so close to doing the same.

"Holy shit, I'm going to cum," she rushes out, her words so breathy, so desperate that my entire body feeds off them, eating them alive, hungry for every sound out of her mouth.

"Yes," I growl, my voice so rough. "Cum for me, let me listen to every fucking noise you make," I moan, and she does. She lets loose, her orgasm ripping through her while she moans into the phone. The sound of her voice fills the entirety of my room, and it sets mine off, forcing me over the edge, too.

I groan into the phone, needing her to hear that I'm right there with her, that I feel the exact same, completely overtaken, completely consumed. This wasn't supposed to be this good. This was supposed to feel like scratching an itch, but I may be addicted now because as my cock leaks cum, my hand continues to stroke, and the only thought on my mind is that I need to do this again, experience this again with her, because this was better than half of the sex I've had, and she didn't even freaking touch me.

We are both just breathing into the phone, that being the only sound in the room. I stare down at the mess I made, knowing I should probably hop in the shower before bed, something I wasn't planning on doing before she called me.

"Jesus Christ, I'm a fucking mess over here," I mutter. I want to hear her voice again. It already feels like it has been too long.

"Me too," she says with a small laugh, and I smile against my phone, wishing for the hundredth time that she was here, that this was a hookup instead of phone sex because then I could hold her, could smell her hair, wrap myself around her, and use her to ground myself.

I know I'm being soft. I know I'm thinking about this too much. But, for me, hookups have never been just about sex. They are about connection, even if it's only for a night. I love cuddling afterward, holding the woman I slept with, even if we both know it is going to end tomorrow. It isn't about something lasting forever, but I'm not just here for a quick physical release. I'm here to feel something with another person, to feel close and intimate, at least for a little while.

"If you were here, I'd carry you to the shower, clean both of us off, and maybe start round two while I held you under the warm spray," I say with a smile in my voice. I feel that I've learned something, feeling as if I am using her lessons and putting them to practice.

"Look at you, what a quick study," she murmurs, her voice low. She sounds sleepy like this has drained her.

"You should get to sleep," I say, a yawn taking over. I'm tired too, needing to be up for work early tomorrow, needing to do about a hundred things, but I know I'm only going to be able to think about this, this night, this orgasm, this woman.

"Yeah, I probably should," she replies, her voice blissful.

"You should call me again tomorrow," I say before I even have a chance to think. I don't second guess my words. I just go with my gut. I just go with the fact that I know I'm gonna want this again: this ease and this desire. This was more than I expected it to be, and if we lived in the same city, I would say that we should just hook up, and become something to each other, even if it was only fuck buddies. But she is too far away, and even being fuck buddies feels like it's off the table for us.

"I don't want a relationship," she says with what sounds like a grimace, as if she hates giving me this news, turning me down.

"Who said I'm asking for a relationship?" I ask, wishing I could explain myself. I also don't have time for a relationship, much less with someone so far away. This right here, this feels like something special, though, and I think we would be stupid to walk away tonight. I don't care if we stay fuck buddies, people who call each other only when we want an orgasm and a little bit of intimacy, but there is something here, something more than just one night, and I know in my core, I want to explore it. "Think of it as a vacation fling, just over the phone," I say. I just want her to agree, to see where I'm coming from, and for her to feel this too.

I listen to her think. The silence fills the speaker, and I can imagine her biting her lip, thinking things through, and trying to figure out what the best thing to do is. I wait, as patiently as I can, trying to give her the space. If she says no, I'll respect it. I'll respect whatever she says because as much as I enjoyed this, I know we can both find people that are closer…people who are easier. On the other hand, I also know that I've found someone I connect with sexually, and the idea of listening to her come apart every night, her orgasm being the last thing I hear before I fall asleep, sounds like fucking heaven.

"I'll call you tomorrow," she finally concedes, a small smile in her voice. "But that's all I'm promising. I don't want a relationship in general, much less with a man a plane ride away," she says, her voice stern. "I don't mind the idea of another orgasm, though, especially if next time, you tell me all the things *you* want to do," she says, her voice getting breathy again, and part of me wants to do it now, wants to use this mess I've made all over myself as lube, and have both of us cum again, but I'm not going to push my luck. I am not going to ask for more than I've already got.

"Works for me," I reply, smiling, and we both hang up, with promises to call tomorrow. I hop out of bed with a stupid fucking grin on my face. I need a shower to clean myself up after one of the best orgasms I've had in a while.

Chapter 8

Avery

I wake up feeling more rested than I have in a long time. It eases my anxiety about it all. I made the decision last night to continue this with Reid, and I'm trying not to freak out about it. The orgasms are good for me. I sleep better, feel better, when someone other than myself is giving me orgasms, and that right there was enough to sway my decision.

I'm uneasy about starting anything long-term with anyone, especially with someone long distance. I don't want the lines to get blurred, making this harder than it needs to be, but his proposal was too good to pass up. The idea of having him on the phone every night while I'm here, helping me cum, talking me through it, was too tempting.

There's also this comfort with us, this ease. He's across the country, not right next door. There is so little risk, such a small chance that this goes wrong. He's connected to Finn, and that might make it complicated, but the odds are, I won't have to see him again, so going forward with this, making it more of a thing than a one-off, doesn't scare me as much as it probably should.

The day is relaxing, calm, but it drags on. The anticipation is killing me, knowing that once I get to my room, once I settle in for the night, I'm gonna have someone to talk to, someone to feel good with. I haven't had this in so long.

Things just feel different with him. Most men want me to do all the work, and even though last night, I was the one putting in the effort, trying to teach him how to have phone sex, he was right there with me, participating, joining in whenever he could, taking an active role in what was happening.

I tuck in earlier than I should, and Emma gives me a confused look as I rise from the lounger, stretching like I'm tired, putting on a show so that she will believe me. She looks at me like she knows something else is going on and knows I'm not just tired. I don't explain though and just give her a vague excuse, pack up quickly, and tuck and run, not wanting her to read it all over my face. She knows me too well for me to lie, but if I can avoid her questions, I can keep my secret as long as I need to.

I pull out my phone on the walk back, the sun setting as I leave the pool, and instantly open the text thread between me and Reid, my fingers moving quickly, my nipples already aching in my bikini top. Something about the promise of sex, knowing it is coming, knowing all day, that it was just a matter of time, has fried my nerves, and made my entire body stiff with desire.

Call me, I'm fucking horny.

I type out the message and hit send, not second-guessing my words. I want to keep things easy, for him to know exactly what I want, and what I need. I don't need to beat around the bush, pretending that I don't want his voice on the phone. I might not want a relationship, but I have no problem asking for sexual pleasure, asking for someone to make me cum. I have no problem putting my needs first, and I'm planning to for the rest of this perfect vacation.

The phone rings while I'm in the elevator, and I hit accept right away, not giving a moment to hold off, not wanting to play those games with him, not caring if he knows I'm eager.

"Hello?" I ask, my voice light, breathy, my desire so transparent. Usually, I'm not like this. Usually, I am the cool one, the one who doesn't care, but I've been thinking about this all day. My body is aching, and my mind is whirling with all the ways this could go tonight. My desire is too high for me to be cool, calm, or collected right now. I'm too horny for that.

"You're a forward one, aren't you?" he asks. There is a smirk in his voice which is so clear I can almost see it. I smile too, enjoying the flirty energy between us. We have had chemistry from the start since our eyes locked in that ballroom, since I saw him checking me out the first time.

"I just know what I want," I murmur as the elevator door opens in front of me, and I walk through, finding my room quickly, shoving the key card in the door, watching the little light on the lock turn green, and I enter.

"And what is it that you want?" he asks, his voice like honey running down my body. I'm too horny for this. I'm gonna embarrass myself. I've been on edge all fucking day, waiting for this, needy for it. I feel like a high schooler, desperate for a boy to even touch me. I hate and love it at the same time. The excitement is euphoric, making my body feel alive, but I hate giving this to him, this desire, this longing, and it makes me want to see his own reaction more, to see how badly *he* wants this too.

"Oh no, I did that last night. Now it's your turn tell me what you want," I purr, laying on my bed, leaving my bikini on for now.

"Oh, is that so?" he asks, his voice drawn out. God, he should not influence me like this. He should not have this much control over my body already, but I'm so fucking horny.

"Yes," I say, my back against the comforter, my breathing coming out faster than normal. I try to calm down, try not to show my cards, but I feel like he knows just based on his voice, on the smugness radiating off of him through the phone.

"Eager little thing tonight, huh?" he asks, a laugh stuck in his throat as he tries to hold back. I squirm around a little, his words having an effect on me, even if he isn't trying. It's a little degrading to be this horny, for him to have this power over me, but it turns me on more, makes my body come alive with lust, and makes my nipples harden in my tiny swimsuit, desperate to be touched.

"I haven't had regular sex in months..." I mumble, trying to explain my way out of this feeling, trying to make it feel a little less embarrassing. "I think my body is just excited to have orgasms multiple days in a row. Don't worry, it'll go away in a few days," I say, holding my cards close to my chest, needing him to be reminded that this won't last. My body is just needy, desperate for a little release, and one night wasn't enough. By the time we are halfway through the week, I'll be over this.

"Sure," he replies, a small smile in his voice, a desire there too, a desperation that matches mine. "So, I'm supposed to lead this one then?" he asks, his voice rough, gravelly. I feel my body respond, wanting this. I feel the comforter behind me, the fabric against the back of my legs, against my ass peeking out from my bikini bottoms. I feel my every nerve ending, and I wish he was here to touch me.

"Yes, just tell me what you would do if you were here, how you would touch me, how you would make me feel, how you'd make me cum," I murmur as I close my eyes against the light in the room, letting my body feel everything a little deeper, stronger with one of my senses gone.

"If I was there right now…" he says, and some shuffling from the other end comes through my speaker. I hope it's him taking off his pants, him getting naked for me, but I'm not a hundred percent sure. I don't know what he's doing, if he's touching himself yet, if he's naked in bed with me in his ear, or if he's holding off, teasing himself, forcing himself to wait until he hears me moan, hears me start to touch myself. That mystery makes my entire body come alive, as I listen for any hint of what he is doing. "I would start with kissing you, settling between your legs, and taking my time," he mutters, his voice low, sultry.

I make an encouraging sound, running my hand up and down my stomach, teasing myself as he speaks to me as he breathes heavily into his phone. I snake my hand down my stomach, my skin erupting into goosebumps at the soft touch, and my head tips back, desire coursing through me. I skim into the bottoms of my bikini, my fingers trailing over the sensitive skin, but I hold off, needing this to last, needing to make this pleasure go on for as long as I can. I finally dip farther down, bringing my fingers to my clit, pressing down on the most sensitive part of my body, and I feel pleasure wrap around me already, my body begging for more.

"I'd have you begging, have your writhing against me. Doing whatever you can for me to touch you, but I wouldn't. I'd just kiss you, just rub against your tight little body until you were going crazy, your pussy fucking dripping for me," he says, his voice so deep, so fucking gravelly that it does things to me. God, imagining him on the other end of this phone, stroking his cock while I moan for him, pleasuring himself with only the sound of my voice and the visual of me doing the exact same thing, makes me so fucking hot.

"Jesus Christ, you're a quick study," I mutter, rubbing small circles in my clit, trying to hold off, trying not to get myself close too fast, but it's hard when my body has been primed for this, desperate for this. I haven't had enough orgasms lately, and now I have the sexiest man on the other end of the phone, breathing heavily, moaning in my ear, and I can't hold myself back.

"I know how to dirty talk, baby, just didn't know women enjoyed it so much over the phone," he mutters, groaning, his voice strained. "Tell me how wet you are," he demands, his voice hard. "Stretch that fucking cunt around your fingers and tell me if you're dripping onto your bedsheets yet. Are you making a fucking mess in that goddamn hotel room?"

I think I literally whimper into the phone, my back arching off the bed. This is too good. It's like fucking audio porn, something I love. Having a man on the other end, moaning so loudly for me, holding nothing back, is like a drug, making my entire body fill with lust.

I do as he says, bringing my fingers down, regrettably leaving my clit, and thrusting one inside of myself, feeling how drenched I am and how needy this pussy is. I add another, needing to be filled, needing to pretend that it's him fucking me with his fingers.

"I'm really fucking wet," I moan, my fingers fucking me, teasing my body, my clit aching to my touched so I bring my palm down, grinding it against myself, and the sensation is almost too much, almost too much good, almost too much stretching, almost too much fucking, but it's so good, too good. "Are you jerking off?" I ask, needing to know, needing to know exactly how he is feeling right now if this is as good for him as it is for me.

"Baby," he groans, and I feel my stomach fill with butterflies, the name making my skin feel extra sensitive. I've never been one for pet names, never wanted to be called something that is only for relationships, but hearing it out of his mouth, hearing him groan out the word, is like a drug, and I'm desperate for another hit. "I don't think I could sit here with you moaning like this and not stroke my cock."

I mewl into the phone, desperation taking all of my senses, taking all of my willpower, all of my self-control, and crushing it. I grind against my palm mercilessly, not giving myself a second to stop, to think. I just do whatever feels good, whatever brings me closer to the edge I am trying to chase.

I want this so badly, but the second that I cum, the second that this pleasure is done, I know it will be time to get off the phone and go to bed, so although I have never wanted anything more, never been more turned on in my goddamn fucking life, I slow with desperation for this to last as long as humanly possible, desperate for more and more and more.

"Don't hold out on me now, baby," he says, a small chuckle escaping him. I hear the wet sounds of his cock, just barely as he strokes it, as he glides his hand up and down his shaft, and wish like nothing more that I could see him, that I was there, sitting beside him while he jerks off, giving him a visual to put with this fantasy.

"I'm trying not to cum," I breathe out, not knowing how much longer I'm going to be able to hold myself off, how much longer I'm going to be able to grind against my hand with my fingers inside of my cunt, with his fucking voice on the other end and not cum, not give in to this intense pleasure.

"Jesus fucking Christ," he rasps out like my words have affected him so much, like he's barely holding on, just like I am. "Fuck, I want to hear you cum. I swear to god, I'm barely lasting as is. I need it," he says through gritted teeth, and it is almost enough to send me over the edge, but I hang on. I'm not really sure why. Maybe pure stubbornness, maybe a desire for him not to know how much he influences me, but I slow down, my back arching off the bed as I try like hell to stop myself from cumming, to stop the waves of pleasure from completely consuming me.

"Jesus. I said fucking cum, Avery. If I was there, you wouldn't have a fucking choice. I'd hold you down and force you to cum, taking your orgasm all for myself," he grits out, and that's it, that's all I can take. The idea of him holding my body down as he forces me to cum, as he wrings pleasure out of me, not giving me a second to breathe, not giving me a break, just forcing me to cum, over and over and over again, sends me right over the edge, into pure bliss.

I hear him at the edge of my senses, encouraging me, praising me as he listens to my noises taking over the hotel room, coming out of me without my consent. I don't have any choice, my body is just responding, pulsing around my fingers as I grind into my palm, desperate to soak up as much of this as I can.

"Good girl, good fucking girl," he praises as I slowly start to come down, as I slowly start to come back to myself. He moans into the phone, and I whimper, my body starting to get overstimulated, my movements starting to be too much. "Don't stop, Avery. You don't get to stop until I cum, and I'm not fucking there yet," he groans out, and I keep moving, my body literally jerking against my hand, overstimulation running through me, but I don't even think about stopping, don't even think about cutting this short.

I push through it, slowing and going softer, but never stopping, listening to his words, listening to him praise me as he curses through his jerking, as I listen to wet sounds of his hand stroking his cock on the other end of the line, and I imagine what would happen if I was there, imagine all the ways he would have me on my back, cumming on his cock, cumming on his face, cumming on his fingers.

Slowly, so fucking slowly, my pleasure starts again, starting at the base of my spine and starting to grow. I've never been one to cum twice, usually satisfied with one orgasm, and no one has ever gone for multiple, never tried to do more than they needed, but as I start to moan again, I hear Reid groan too, listening to me pleasure myself again, listen to me build up again, my orgasm already too close after I just came, after my back arched off the goddamn bed, holding me hostage to the pleasure.

"God, you sound so fucking good, Avery," he groans out, his voice deep, and I imagine him desperate for release, right on the edge, his cock leaking pre-cum, but keeping himself there, wanting me to get there with him again, wanting me to cum with him. I set the phone beside my head, putting it on speaker, bringing my hand to my bikini top, moving it aside quickly, feeling my tits in my hand, feeling my hard nipples against my palm, pinching, tugging, desperate for more.

"Jesus Christ, I might cum again," I mutter, wanting to see if my theory is correct, if he wants me to cum again, if he gets off on my pleasure, gets off on knowing that I'm enjoying this. I hear his movements slow, as if he is holding himself back, and he curses into his phone, the sound running down my body like he is here, touching me.

"Yes, cum again. Oh my god, cum again. I need to hear it," he mumbles, his words starting to lose meaning as my pussy starts to clench, my body tensing every single muscle. I come alive under his voice, my pleasure building quicker than it should, quicker than it ever has, finding pleasure in him, in his voice, in his desperation. "I need you to cum again. I need to fucking hear it," he groans, his voice so breathy, so desperate. The hint of him begging makes me fucking gush, my fingers wet with my arousal. I love that sound, the sound of bringing a powerful man to his knees, making him desperate for me.

I lean into his words, not thinking, not giving myself a moment to second guess, to wonder if another orgasm is even possible. I just listen to him, letting my body do its job, and I feel myself start to cum, my entire body tense, my back bowing off the bed, and I moan into the phone, unable to stop myself, unable to take a breath, the pleasure being too all-consuming.

"Fuck, fuck, fuck, Avery," Reid groans, his sounds the only thing registering as I desperately try to come back down to earth, as my pleasure starts to ebb. I try to catch my breath, my chest moving violently, my legs still shaking, my entire body stiff from tensing every single one of my muscles.

"Oh fuck, I'm cumming," Reid groans into the phone. "Holy fuck." I can hear the exact second his load shoots from his cock, his sounds being a play-by-play of what is happening, his groans becoming stronger as he comes apart. I wish I was there, wish I was on the receiving end of his cum, wish I was watching his face, looking into his eyes as he orgasms, as bliss takes him over.

We don't speak for a few seconds, both of us just catching our breath. I stare at the ceiling, my brain barely even working. I barely even feel like a person, but one thought keeps bouncing around in my head, and I wonder if he has the same thought as me, that I can't believe how good that was, can't believe how this phone sex is better than the sex I've had with most of my past partners. I can't believe how hard I came, and I wonder if he feels this too, this chemistry, this desperation for more. I've just came twice, both harder than most of my orgasms, and I want more, want more of this, want more pleasure, which is something I shouldn't even be capable of anymore, but it feels like he just unleashed something inside of me, this desperate need, this desire that has been unbottled, and now it's overflowing, begging for more.

"Fuck," he said, a smile in his voice. He rustles around, moving on the other end of the phone, and then seems to settle back into bed, the line silent for a few seconds.

My brain starts to work again, my body starting to really come back to itself. A question nags at the back of my head, something that has bugged me since he said it, but I wasn't sure if I wanted to ask, if I wanted the answer to my question. Yet, after that orgasm, after what happened between us, it feels like I could ask him anything, feels like a sort of trust has built up around us, and during my post orgasm haze, I feel bold. I feel like anything I say doesn't count right now, doesn't count while we are still catching our breath.

"Why did you ask if I was a brat yesterday?" I ask, breaking the comfortable silence, my question being the only sound on the line for a few seconds. I wonder if my question is going to make this awkward, going to make this delicate thing between us break, if the sudden peace I've been able to find in him and the phone sex will poof away, leaving me a horny mess in its absence.

"Usually, I have a radar for those kinds of things," he says, his voice hesitant, as if he knows this is more than just a simple question. "I'm usually right, though," he says, a lightness to his tone, as if he knows me better than I know myself, but he isn't sure how I'm going to take it.

Honestly, maybe he does have me figured out more than I do because I've never even considered something like that. I've slept with so many men who want me to do the work, who want me to suck their cock, ride them, make them cum over and over and over again, pleasing them in ways they couldn't even begin to please me. They made me cum, made sure that I finished, but it was always me doing so much work, calling the shots. I haven't thought about doing anything else or what it would feel like to give up control, to let someone else into the driver's seat and see where we end up.

"So you still think I'm a brat," I ask, my voice giving my smile away as curiosity replaces my anxiety. If there is a person who I could experiment with and try something like that, it would be him. I shift on the bed, sitting up, putting my bikini back together so I'm not just sitting here naked. I pull the covers away, settling under them, and getting comfortable.

"I can't tell you what you are. Only you know that, but you give the energy of a brat, at least in my opinion." His answer only causes more questions inside of me, only stokes the curiosity that is brewing.

"And what is a brat by your definition?" I ask, my interest piqued.

"Someone who wants to be dominated, wants to be told what to do but likes to fight it. Usually, brats don't just comply. They like to fight a little," he says, his voice moving down an octave, and I feel the shift between us, this calm shifting into energy, into electricity.

"Isn't that annoying? Doesn't a dom want to tell them what to do?" I ask, licking my lips, suddenly parched, my entire body on edge. I can feel my nipples starting to harden, my body starting to come back alive, even after the orgasms. I don't know how he does this, has me so on edge at all times, ready for pleasure.

"Usually a little bit of fight means a lot of punishment. It's not the same for everyone. Everyone likes something different, but I love giving out punishments, making someone submit, getting them to finally give me all the control, even though I know they are hesitant," he admits, and I want to touch myself, want to please myself as we talk about this, want to try to be quiet, so he can't hear me, but I want a moan to slip, letting him know exactly what I'm doing.

I push that urge down, though, trying to stay focused, trying not to let my horny brain take over.

"Why do you like that?" I ask, my voice so fucking breathy, giving away every ounce of my desire. Reid groans lightly, moving the sound into clearing his throat, like he knows how much this conversation is influencing me, how turned on my body is, but he keeps talking, keeps answering my questions like we both don't know how much this is turning me on.

"It's a level of trust, I think. Giving your power to someone, letting them make all the decisions, there's this huge level of vulnerability. It requires trust that you know them, know what they like, what they *need,*" he says the last word low, almost on a growl, and I hold back my own moan, wanting nothing more than to have him know exactly what I need and have him give it to me, taking every ounce of thought from my head.

"That's interesting," I reply softly, my brain not working fast enough to come up with another good question. I'm too consumed in the lust, in the idea of him being here, telling me exactly what to do, tying me up, using my body exactly how he wants, pleasuring me as much as he can, giving me everything I have ever wanted, everything I have ever *needed.*

"God, your pussy is so fucking needy, isn't it?" he asks, his words barely registering before my eyebrows shoot up, my entire body shocked by his words. I bite my lip, trying to keep my reaction, trying to keep how hot his words are to myself, but it's hard when he's right there, when he can hear my breath, can hear every intake of air into my lungs. "Two orgasms wasn't enough for you?" he chides. "That's okay, baby. Play with your greedy pussy. I'll stay on the phone until you're satisfied," he says, his voice so low again, and I gulp, my pussy literally throbbing, literally begging him for it, desperate for him to hear me while I cum for the third time.

"I–I," I stumble, not even knowing how to reply. This feels so different than when I was teaching him, like a new man is on the phone with me, not the same man that was there yesterday, and I have to admit, I'm so much hornier for this guy, so much more desperate for him. "I already came twice," I respond, not fully knowing why that matters, but it seems too much for me to want to cum again, for me to be this desperate for more pleasure. It feels selfish to want more, to want him to sit here while I cum again, even though I know that's irrational, stupid even, thinking he wouldn't enjoy it just as much as I would.

"Avery," he says sternly, like a command in and of itself, and I squeeze my thighs together, licking my lips again. I wish he could see me, wish he knew how insane he is driving me. "Is your pussy dripping on the sheets right now?" he asks, his voice condescending, like he already knows the answer, already knows exactly what I'm going to say.

And the answer, of course, is yes. I'm so horny. Hornier than I have ever been, and I just came twice, once more than I usually, do, and yet I'm fucking aching for a third. I can't imagine not cumming again, not giving myself this, but anxiety pricks in the back of my mind, keeping me from touching myself, keeping me from pleasing myself.

"I've already kept you on the phone for too long. You should probably go to bed. I'll just take care of this myself," I mutter, not knowing where this is coming from, not knowing why the idea that he wants this, wants to listen to me cum is so insane to me.

"Avery, I wasn't asking. I'm literally leaking pre-cum all over myself. I'm making such a fucking mess for you, and you aren't even here to clean it up, so the least you could do is cum for me again," he groans out. It sounds as though his teeth are clenched. I feel my eyebrows shoot up, his words doing nasty things to me, making my entire body feel like a live wire, desperate for more, and I finally give in, giving myself more, giving myself exactly what I need.

I bring my hand back down under my bikini and start rubbing my throbbing clit, needing more, needing his words to be true, needing to be able to put my trust in him that he wants this just as badly as I do.

"Holy fuck," I moan out, my body firing, every single one of my cells screaming for more, screaming for an orgasm. I can't believe how good this feels, how intense this pleasure is. Hearing Reid's voice on the other end helps quite a bit, hearing his praise, his own moans, his hand fucking his cock again, the wet sounds radiating through my phone, my back arching off the bed, and I get closer and closer to orgasm.

I would think it would take longer to cum after two orgasms, after getting what I thought was my fill, but Reid guides me through it, talking to me, moaning for me, telling me that I'm doing such a good job, telling me how much he wishes he was here to be the one who is pleasuring me. It only takes a few minutes of playing with my clit until I'm right on the fucking edge, seconds away from falling over it again.

I wait, though, for what I'm not sure, but I hold off, keeping myself from cumming.

"I'm so fucking close," I whine, my entire body begging for it, trying to push me over the edge, trying to get me to cum. Still, I hold myself off, teasing the fuck out of myself, wanting his permission, wanting him to tell me what to do, take the thought away from me, and take every ounce of control that I am offering.

"God, baby, fucking cum already, you're driving me insane." His words register in my mind, his confirmation, and I feel myself fall off the edge, my vision going hazy as pleasure wraps around me. It's so powerful, so all-consuming, that I can't even think for a second, can't even pretend to be present on this earth. I know I'm moaning, know I'm making noise, but it doesn't feel like me, doesn't feel like I'm even inside of my own body, but when I finally start to resurface, finally start to come back to earth, my voice feels a little raw, my throat a little dry, and I know all that noise was me.

"You are fucking dangerous, you know that?" he asks, and I blink out of my haze, blink away the lust washing through me. That was a whole new experience, a whole new kind of orgasm. I was so turned on, so horny that it wasn't even something I had experienced before.

"You are the one that just made me cum harder than I ever have. I think you might be the dangerous one," I retort, breathless. I suck in air, desperate for it, as if I was deprived for hours, and I'm finally getting a taste again.

"God, I wish I was there," he moans out, his voice desperate, longing, a hint of something deeper, a hint of something close to adoration. I don't look too hard at that, though, not wanting to see something I'm not ready for.

"Me too," I say with a yawn, my body completely wrung out, every nerve cell drained, desperate to sleep after three orgasms. I'm not used to cumming so many times, not used to taking every ounce of pleasure that I can, of using my body so thoroughly, but I love the weightlessness to my bones, the calm running through me, making it feels so easy to sink into sleep.

"Get some sleep. I'll call again tomorrow," Reid says, yawning himself as if he is just realizing what time it is.

"You are the one who needs to get up for work tomorrow," I say, my eyes closing, the desire to just sink into my blankets is overpowering me, overpowering my desire to put on pajamas and brush my teeth before sleep. I just want to let go, let this feeling overtake me, and become one with the bed.

"I may be tired tomorrow, but it was worth it to hear you cum three times," he groans out, and I feel myself start to sink, not even having the energy to reply, to explain to him how fucking good this was, how much I want to do this again, how much this scares me, this chemistry we have. "Get some sleep," he says, but he feels far away, and I know sleep already has me, so I let myself sink, not hearing the beep of the call ending, not knowing if he hung up, but weirdly enjoying the idea that he is still right there, waiting for me on the other line.

Chapter 9

Reid

I stayed on the phone too late last night, just listening to Avery's soft snoring sound. I listened to her roll around every now and again, imagining that we were there together, that I was in her bed.

I should have just hung up right away. I'm sure she wouldn't enjoy the fact that I stayed on like a teenager. I just wanted to soak up a few more minutes with her. She has made it clear what she wants. This isn't going to go any farther than a fling. I'm doing my best to respect that, but it's hard when I want nothing more than to convince her to fly here. I want her to let me use her body. I want to spend time with her between my sheets and then, spend time getting to know her. I want to learn all about her and all the things that make her tick.

It's not even just about the sex. I mean, that part is great, and would probably be better if we didn't have distance in our way, but it's so much more than that. She keeps surprising me. She keeps giving me a level of trust that I'm not sure I deserve. She is funny and so fucking sexy. I find myself wanting to stay on the phone with her for just a few extra minutes, enjoying every second I can.

But she doesn't want that. She doesn't want to figure out if this thing between us could ever be more. I need to be better at respecting that. I need to be okay with just having a week of her on the other end of the phone and nothing more.

Work goes by slowly for most of the day. I barely make it to lunchtime with my eyes open, handling about a hundred meetings and reviewing our quarter financials. They all seem more pointless when I'm exhausted. It all feels like just another way to waste company time. I push through them, needing to get through this day and nap before I'm on the phone again tonight.

A little after lunch, I'm sitting at my desk, wondering if I really need to be here or if this wouldn't be a good day to just go home early and get some extra sleep. My phone vibrates with a text. All of my clients and my assistant, have my number so when the vibration moves through the room, I hold back a groan. I don't have the energy to deal with another person right now.

But when I look down, I'm pleasantly surprised. Avery's name lights up my phone. I feel myself smile. But I try to stifle it and try to convince myself that I didn't show any emotion over her message. I've never been really good at hiding how I feel, though.

Is it bad that I woke up horny, even after last night?

This time, I do groan. My self-control is melting in front of me, making the idea of doing more work or actually being productive even less appealing.

Avery is more than I bargained for. I mean that in the best fucking way possible. When we first talked at the bar, I thought she would be a good time, a one-night thing to scratch the itch that has been bugging me for the last few months.

I want a relationship. I always have. I'm not one of those men who hate commitment or don't know how to settle with one woman. To me, that idea sounds like heaven, having some-one to come home to, to go to for support, to lean on, and to lean on me. Relationships mean a comfort, desire, and trust that isn't like anything else. So I want a relationship. Yet, even I wasn't considering that when I met Avery. I just wanted to see where the night would take us. Now though, I can feel myself getting more and more fucked. I'm getting more and more attached.

She is insatiable. She's so fucking horny, so desperate anytime I tell her what to do. I think she just doesn't know that she's kinky. It feels like something she has yet to explore. The fact that she is doing it with me, giving me her trust, speaks volumes and makes me like her just a little more.

Not even a little. In fact, you're making my day about a hundred times harder now that I know that information.

I type out the message and hit send. I put my phone off to the side, planning on actually getting some work done, intent on going home a little early today. Then, my phone pings with a response. I can't help myself. I pick it back up and read her message like a fiend.

I have another lesson for you...

I stare at the message for a second. I'm not sure what she is getting at. Another message pops up. This one a photo. I feel my eyebrows raise, my entire body tensing as I stare at the image of her tits. Her bikini is just barely pulled off to the side, so her nipples peek out. She is grabbing one of them, pinching her nipple between her fingers, and I groan lightly, thinking about her in bed, in a hotel room, playing with herself while I'm stuck all the way over here. Another message pops up, moving the picture higher, taking a fourth of the image away from me.

Photos make everything a little more interesting ;) send me something back so I can make myself cum? I can't wait until tonight.

I bring my hand up and run it down my face, trying like hell to keep ahold of my self-control. It is not a good idea to send her a picture from my office or to sext her while I'm at work. Yet, the desire to please her, for her cum while looking at my cock, looking at only images of me, is consuming. It makes all of my capability for rational thought fly out the window.

God, you know last night when I called you dangerous? This is what I meant.

Chapter 10

Avery

The longer I talk to Reid, the slower the days go. I seem to be planning my entire day waiting for night, trying to get myself in bed as soon as possible without raising suspicion. My sister knows me too well, and I'm shocked she hasn't figured out I'm hooking up with someone yet. I want to tell her, want to give her every juicy detail, but I'm not sure if I'm ready yet. She knows him, knows what I'm getting into more than I do, and I hate that. I don't want her opinions, don't want her commentary before I've even had a chance to figure out what this is myself, to figure out exactly what I want from it.

The sun finally sets, finally dips below the line, leaving the pool in darkness, the sun taking my hope of a tan with it. I have been in the sun more this week than I have in the past five years, and although I have almost gone through an entire bottle of sunscreen, I've been enjoying it more than I care to admit. Getting away from the city, around some of the bloodsuckers that live there, has been peaceful, a little too much so.

I can feel myself getting comfortable. The days spent in the sun with my sister, the nights spent with Reid. It's just all so easy, such a nice existence and a part of me hates it, hate how easy it is for me to sink into. This won't last, won't stay forever, and when I have to go back to work, I know I'm gonna miss the hell out of this.

I sigh, feeling off-kilter, weirdly feeling like I've lost the balance in my life. I have worked so hard to make a life for myself, so hard to push myself to be something, to be all of the success I could ever need. This was my one break, one time in my life I was going to take a breath. I thought it would make me feel better, make me feel excited to get back to work, get back to my cozy life, but all it does is fill me with dread, the idea that this isn't my life, that this can't go on forever. I want time to stop, leaving me here, letting me live here forever.

I keep such a handle on my life, trying my best to do everything I'm supposed to, keeping myself out of distractions, but all of these distractions, the drinking, the tanning, the phone sex, have made my life outside of this, feel dull, giving me a sense of uncertainty.

I know life can't always be like this, fun and drinks and sex, but as I'm leaving the pool, I feel a sense of happiness I haven't had before, having experienced. I feel calm, at peace, like my life is starting to click together, and as much as I'm enjoying myself, it just makes me realize that it wasn't clicked together before, wasn't where I needed to be.

I hate how everything has changed in the matter of a few days, made my old life seem boring and bleak, but I know the best way to distract myself, know the best way to forget all about this, to lose all control. At least, I'm starting to know it, starting to learn how to give control to Reid. I want that now, to stop thinking, to stop considering all the ways my life is going wrong, all the ways I wish things were different. I want to forget, want to lose every thought inside of my head, and I know he is the perfect person for that.

I make my way up to my room quickly, needing the distraction, needing something to ground me more than I expected. I have never felt like this, felt so uneasy about my life, and although maybe I should look closer at the feeling, it's too overwhelming, too much for me to handle, and the idea of being distracted, of having a man distract me while making me cum, is just too tempting.

My phone is ringing as soon as I close the door. I am a few minutes earlier than we had planned. After our midmorning nude sending, which led to me cumming and him having to hold back since he was at work. We agreed on a time, setting a date. It made my resolve slip, my determination to keep this casual, to keep feelings out of the equation. The idea of setting a time, of having consistent plans with someone made me smile, made me giddy, but I'm sure it's just the multiple orgasms, just having someone to rely on to pleasure me when I need it most.

"You're early," Reid's voice vibrates through the phone. I smile lightly as the door clicks shut behind me, and I make my way over to my bed, feeling like a schoolgirl on the phone with her crush. I plop down on the bed, my nerves running wild, making my body feel all jittery.

"I call it punctual," I say with a small laugh, loving and hating that he has me found out, that he called me out on wanting to talk to him a little bit early. He has done it in such a funny way that it makes me feel like he almost enjoys it, enjoys that I want to talk to him, enjoys that I called early, like he was waiting for me.

"I call it horny. You got a taste, and now you can't stay away, huh?" he asks, and I feel my cheeks heat, suddenly happy that he is hundreds of miles away because his words have a level of truth, an undeniable level of honesty.

"I don't know if I would go that far," I retort. "You seemed to enjoy my pictures today, though. And let's be honest, you picked up the phone. You must be a little horny too," I say, needing to take the attention off of me and how much I'm enjoying this, having someone to end my night with.

"Guilty," he answers, his voice light, but what he is saying feels so strong. I know it shouldn't, but it does. We are saying that we wanted to talk to each other, that we were both waiting, desperate for the other, and it feels oddly intimate.

"So I was thinking we could try something new," Reid says, breaking the silence, bringing us back on track for the entire reason I called.

"What's that?" I ask, clearing my throat, trying to get my mind back in the place we both want it to be.

"I was reading up on it a little bit, and a lot of people do like a guided thing, where they tell their partner exactly what to do. So I was thinking we could try that," he says softly, with a confident undertone, like he isn't sure how I'm going to respond but wants me to know that he wants this. I try to process his thoughts, but my mind catches on his first words, not letting them go.

"Wait... You've been reading up on what?" I ask, not fully understanding, convinced that he can't mean what I think he does.

"Phone sex," he says as if it is simple, as if it means nothing, but instead, I find it so fucking endearing.

"You were reading up on phone sex?" I ask, completely dumbfounded, shocked that he would go to such lengths. "Why?" I finally ask, wanting more, trying not to make assumptions, wanting to hear it from him, why he would do something so thoughtful.

"Because I want it to be the best it can be..." he says, and then after a few seconds, he adds, "For you," he says this part quietly, his voice still so deep like this conversation is turning him on while it's spinning my goddamn head in a circle.

"That is... so fucking sweet, actually?" I say, but it sounds like a question, the end of my sentence lifting in tone and volume, my voice a squeak against my ears. I sit there for a second, the silence taking over, while I think of this extremely handsome man, across the country, who could probably be having actual sex with other people, finding his pleasure in someone else. Instead, he is looking up phone sex, trying to perfect his technique for me. Someone he has only met once, for someone that shouldn't be anything to him... yet, I seem to be.

I don't know why this hits me so hard. I don't know why this makes my chest hurt, because it is simple. He didn't make some big grand gesture, didn't do something that took hours of his time, but it has a level of thoughtfulness that I didn't expect from him, from someone I have been labeling as a vacation fling in my head. I have been so adamant that he can't be anything else. He can't mean more to me than this, but God, he is slowly finding a place in my life, inserting himself where I need him most, and it makes me uneasy while also giving me butterflies.

This is more effort than a majority of my boyfriends have put in, more effort into my enjoyment, into my pleasure. Usually, they just rub my clit and hope I cum, deciding that it is my fault if I don't because they did their best. For Reid, someone who I don't even plan on talking to after a few more days, to go to the effort to find the best ways to make me cum, the best ways to make this experience better, hits me more than it should, more than I want it to.

"I wasn't really going for sweet," he says, his voice a low hum, humor radiating through him. "Extremely sexy, mind-numbingly hot, maybe," he says, and I smile into my phone, feeling close to him, feeling like he is right here, in this room with me, more present with me than anyone else has been, closer to me than I've felt with anyone else before.

"It was also mind-numbingly hot," I say lightly, smiling like a fucking idiot, trying to get myself to stop but failing. I give myself this moment, intent on going back to my resolve tomorrow, going back to this being just a fling when the sun rises. For now, I'm going to soak this up and enjoy it, because I don't have any other choice. It's too good to let go of.

"Good, that's what I was going for," he mutters, his voice so sexy, so intimate. "So, what do you think? I've never done the guided thing, but the idea of you having to listen to everything I say, I have to admit, sounds fucking hot," he says lightly. I like the way we talk about these things, bringing up ideas and having a conversation about them. Things with him are so open, so comfortable, and that's not something I've had before with a boyfriend or a fuck buddy. I'm not used to people so open to talking about sex, talking about what they want, but it is truthfully a breath of fresh air.

"I'm willing to try if you are. If I'm being honest, I need some of the brain-numbing that you keep talking about," I say lightly, not wanting to give too much away, not wanting to confess exactly how I've been feeling these past few days. I want to hold my feelings close to my chest, at least for now, until I figure them out a little more.

"Bad day?" he asks, a seriousness taking him over that warms me from the inside out.

"No, just need to get out of my own head," I say, giving him the half-truth that is safe, the one-sided truth that doesn't make me want to throw up, that doesn't spin my world on its axis.

"I think I can help with that," he says.

I mutter a small "thank God," in response, a smile in my voice, so fucking clearly. Actually, I think I have smiled more with Reid than I have in months. I've been sitting on the phone, smiling for the last few days, so much so that my cheeks are starting to hurt. My face is beginning to use muscles it isn't used to using.

"What are you wearing?" he asks, his voice turning gravelly, deeper than normal, his sex voice coming out.

"My bikini. The same one I was wearing earlier when I sent you those pictures," I say, my voice also going husky, the reminder of what happened this afternoon making my entire body come alive. I sent him pictures of my tits, moving my bikini top to the side, and when he sent me back a bulge picture, evidence of what I do to him, evidence that he is wrapped up in this as much as I am, it swarmed me desire, with a desperation for him to just be here with me.

"I swear that picture is burned into my brain. My cock has been hard all fucking day," he groans out, and I enjoy seeing him in pain over what my body can do to him. It's a sick sense of power, but I bask in it anyway.

"Good," I say softly, liking the idea of him thinking about me all day, of him looking at his phone, over and over again, looking at the picture, not able to stop.

"So, you're going to do everything I say?" he asks, his voice going stern, and it sounds sexy on him. I like the way authority sounds on him. "Yes sir," I say, remembering how much he enjoyed the name last time, and wanting to hear how badly he wants this, wanting his voice to lull me into a sense of security, into a sense of safety, because the other feelings I'm having for him, this need, this desire, to continue whatever the fuck we have started is making anxiety crawl up my spine.

"Fuck," he groans, his voice low. "This is you being a brat. You give me the power to control your body, and yet still, you drive me fucking wild."

"I don't know what you're talking about," I murmur, my voice low, teasing, and I bite my lip, enjoying this feeling, like he may be calling all the shots, but I know I have him wrapped around my finger. He might be in control, but we both know that he only has control, because I've given it to him, something I never considered when it came to these kinds of relationships, where the man takes the lead. I always thought it would feel a little degrading, to let a man tell me what to do, to listen to him, but it almost feels the opposite, like I have more power than I ever have.

"You know, I have half a mind to punish you," he mutters, and I feel a thrill run through me, the idea that he would do that, would make me pay for this control I have over him, is overpowering.

"And how would you do that?" I ask, teasing, pushing him, not knowing if I want the punishment or not, both options sounding a little too sweet.

"I'd sit here, stroking my cock, over and over again, fucking my hand while I think of you, and I'd cum, again and again, and I wouldn't let you touch yourself, not once. I wouldn't let you please that tight little body, wouldn't let that back arch off the bed. I would just make you listen while I cum with your name on my lips," he says, and by the time he is done, my eyes are wide, my clit throbbing, wanting that, but wanting anything else. That sounds like the sweetest torture, the best punishment I've ever heard of.

"And you say *I'm* dangerous," I say, my voice husky, so desperate for everything he described. I didn't know giving power would feel like this, letting a man have control wasn't supposed to be this addicting, but the longer he talks to me, the more I want it, the more I want to experience this life, where I give everything I have and he uses it so expertly, knowing exactly what I need at every given moment.

"You are dangerous. My cock is already leaking pre-cum all over because of you," he says, his voice a growl.

"And that's my fault?" I ask, pushing him, wanting to test his limits.

"Yes. You are sitting there with your big tits and your tight little cunt, and you are so fucking horny for me, but I'm all the way over here. You are *enjoying* teasing me, making me so hard it's unnatural. You know exactly how to drive me crazy," he says, and I can hear the lust in his voice, how badly he wishes he was here with me, that we were fucking instead of resorting to phone sex.

"Then it's your fault that I'm sitting here horny, my cunt just *aching* to be filled," I say, smiling when he groans into the phone, giving me the exact reaction I was hoping for, was looking for when the words came out of my mouth.

"Move your bikini top, just like you did in that photo," he says, his voice suddenly serious, and I feel the power dynamic switch. I feel him take control again, as he gets sick of listening to me be bratty, and I rush to comply, not feeling threatened by him at all, his voice making me feel giddy instead.

"Okay," I say, my voice breathy, and I do what he says, pulling my tits out, the cold air in the room giving me chills, my nipples hardening.

"Play with them, make them fucking ache. Play with them until you are writhing around, wishing I was there to please that ache inside of you." His voice is lethal, doing things to my body that I wasn't even sure could happen, forcing lust into me faster than I am ready for.

I rub my nipples, my tits more sensitive than usual, my entire body primed and ready, desperate for release. With him, foreplay seems to start the second we get on the phone, with the banter and the dirty talk. By the time I actually start to touch myself, I swear I'm dripping and so fucking horny it is making me insane.

I moan as I touch myself, my tits in both my hands, feeling the weight of them, pinching my nipples lightly, letting him hear how good this feels, how badly my body wants this. I do exactly as he asked, needing him to know that I want this, want to give him this control, even if it makes me nervous, even if I'm unsure because this feels better than it should. This feels like something that has been missing, and I'm ready to explore exactly how good it can be when I finally give up the control I've been so desperate to hang onto.

"Good fucking girl, that's right. Tease your fucking body while I stroke my cock," he says, as he groans into the phone, his moans like music to my ears, making my body pulse harder.

I keep listening to him, both of us moaning, but after a while, the ache between my legs feels like too much to ignore, and I'm miserable sitting there, barely able to pleasure myself, barely able to have any relief. I wait for him to tell me what to do next, for him to give me permission to touch myself more, to finally get the same relief that he is, but he doesn't say anything. He leaves me here, with my tits in my hand, my neediness only growing, as I listen to him get closer and closer to orgasm.

"Can–" I start, stopping myself, unsure if I should ask, un-sure how this works, but I'm not sure I can wait any longer. He quiets, giving me a chance to think, a chance to speak. "Can I touch my clit?" I ask, the words feeling unfamiliar in my mouth. I'm not used to asking permission, but when he hums, considering my request, I feel myself rush with desire, with this need to please him, to obey him.

"Are you horny? Desperate for some relief?" he asks, and I'm nodding before he has even finished his sentence, so turned on, my clit is throbbing, begging for touch. I want it so badly. I'm not sure how he got me here, wound so tight, so fucking needy it feels like I can't even take a deep breath, but here I am.

"Yes," I whimper, realizing that he can't see me, can't see how much I'm nodding, how eager I am.

"Well, that's too bad, isn't it? Maybe you should learn not to be such a fucking tease," he says, with a smugness in his voice, as if he is enjoying this. I'm sure he is, if the stroking on the other end is any indication. I can hear each stroke, the wetness coating his cock squelching loudly, giving me a visual every time he thrusts up and down, pleasing himself.

I whine, fucking *whine,* into the phone, not really caring anymore, knowing I sound a little pathetic, needing pleasure more than I need my self-respect.

"Oh, are you really that horny?" he asks, while I keep playing with my tits, getting myself more worked up, hating and loving it at the exact same time. It is the sweetest kind of torture to only be able to play with my nipples, only be able to please myself briefly, but it's not enough. I rub my thighs together, needing something, needing more, but it doesn't do much, doesn't take away the ache.

"Yes!" I exclaim, my filter starting to go out the window, my mind feeling like mush.

"Okay, fine," he murmurs, a hint of mischief in his voice. "Touch your clit, but don't move your fingers," he says softly, but I don't even think before I move. His words don't even process, but the second I touch myself, the second I start to scratch the itch deep within myself, his meaning becomes clear. I freeze my movement, and I make a noise of annoyance, not able to stop myself, not able to keep myself quiet when the only thing going through my head is getting myself to orgasm.

"You're kidding, right?" I ask, getting fed up, my lust clouding every thought inside my mind. I can't think, can't feel, anything other than this. I can barely process the words coming out of my own mouth because I want this so desperately.

"You heard me. You can place your fingers on your clit, but you can't circle it, or stroke it, or move," he says, and my head falls back on a groan. I do what he says, but needing something, anything, needing more friction that I'm currently getting with my tit in my hand, and my clit against my fingers, and although I know it won't be enough, I know I'm going to take whatever I can get.

"I think you're going to kill me," I grind out, my teeth clenched as I push my fingers down, giving myself the tiniest hint of pressure, desperately trying to stay still, trying not to circle my clit, stroke myself to orgasm. It would happen fast too, probably faster than Reid could stop me or tell me not to cum. I'm so close already, wound too fucking tight. It would take nothing to send me over the edge.

"I can hear you thinking through the phone, Avery. Don't even fucking think about it," he says in warning, and I feel myself still, as if he's here, watching me, reading my thoughts.

"I'm not thinking anything," I say breathily, my voice a shock even to myself. I don't know if I've ever been this horny, this desperate for an orgasm, this close to the edge, and forced to just wait, to just hang on and look over the edge but not being allowed to fall.

"You're a brat. I know *exactly* what you're thinking, and if you cum before I tell you to, I swear to God, you'll pay for it," he says, and a thrill runs through me, excitement, curiosity.

"What does that mean exactly?" I ask, my voice too obvious, my entire body thrumming as I wait for him to describe what punishment would be waiting for me. I know it would be good, too good, and it is tempting, tempting to just let go, to let this pleasure consume me and discard everything he is saying.

"I'm not going to tell you. You are so fucking dirty, sitting over there, wanting me to tell you about the nasty things I'm gonna do if you disobey? No fucking way. I'll just say, this wouldn't be a fun punishment, one that you get off on. This one would be torture. I probably wouldn't let you cum for days if I had my way," he says. I gulp lightly, not liking the sounds of that, not liking the sound of him making me suffer for longer than I already have.

"Well, that doesn't sound very fun," I say, my finger itching to move, to please myself, but I hold steady, not wanting to find out what punishment he had in mind, not wanting to be told not to cum for days.

Of course, I could throw everything he says out the window, not listen to even an ounce of it, but this is part of the fun. I'm giving him control, letting him tell me what to do. I'm trusting that he knows my body, knows what is going to make me feel good, even if I don't want to do it. I'm trusting that he will get me out of my own head, get me out of overthinking, and get me into my body, into my lust. It isn't just about control, isn't just about him telling me what to do. I'm seeing that it is so much more than that, and there is much more pleasure to be had than I ever imagined.

"Not every punishment is supposed to be fun for you, ya know?" he asks, a smile in his voice, like he finds me endearing. The way he is talking to me, almost like I am beneath him, like I am someone he needs to train, someone he needs to coach, like he knows so much more than me, shouldn't turn me on. It's slightly patronizing, slightly embarrassing, but super hot at the same time.

"Can I please, make myself cum?" I ask, barely hanging on, this entire situation being a test of my patience that I wasn't prepared for. I'm not sure if I knew what I was getting myself into when this started.

"I think maybe you should be forced to listen to me cum first," he says, and he knows that he got me, knows that he has something over me. That's one of my biggest turn-ons: listening to men moan, listening to the sounds they make, the way the air leaves their lungs like they can't imagine going another second without being inside of you. I've always loved having a man fall to his knees in front of me, so overcome with pleasure, and the idea that he's going to cum, while I sit here, writhing against my own fucking hand, is goddamn torture.

"No, please," I beg. " We can cum at the same time," I try, wanting to hear him cum, wanting to pleasure myself right now, not *after* he cums first. I don't want to have to wait, listen to him as he gets off, and be left a horny fucking mess.

"God, you are so fucking needy. You can't wait a few more minutes?" he asks, and I can hear his smug smile, his enjoyment over how desperate I am. I whine in the back of my throat, warring with myself inside of my head.

"No," I say pathetically, and I feel it, feel how badly my body needs this, how turned on I am. I am consumed by this pleasure. It is taking over every cell inside of my body, taking over every thought inside of my head. Nothing else lives here. No one is home, the lust and the desire have taken residence, and they won't leave until they get what they came for.

"Fine, since you are too horny to wait," he says, like I am inconveniencing him, but in the best way possible. He acts like this is putting him out, like my lust is annoying for him, like he isn't loving this. It's this light level of degradation, yet part of me loves it and is basking in it.

"Ugh, yes, yes, yes, please," I murmur, my words blending together, my clit throbbing against my finger, desperation leaking from my every pore. I have never felt like this, so horny, so fucking needy that I can't even think, can't even breathe. I need to cum, so fucking badly.

"You want to cum?" he asks, and I huff, my annoyance growing, my impatience overtaking me.

"Is that not obvious?" I ask, my tone biting, my body begging to grind against my fingers, begging to move. I hold off, with every ounce of willpower I have, but it's slowly slipping, making it harder and harder to actually listen to what he has to say.

"You have an attitude when you are turned on," he says with a small laugh, and his casualness irritates me, digs into my skin, and makes me angry. I am sitting over here, writhing, and it feels like he is messing with me, playing with my emotions and enjoying every second of it. "Avery?" he asks lightly, his voice breathy, cocky.

"What?" I say through clenched teeth, my pulse ringing through my ears, my hips starting to move, barely thrusting up, just a half inch, my body not able to contain anymore.

"Cum," he says, and I don't waste a second, don't stop to think, don't give my body a moment to ask if I should or if this is okay. I just react to his words, so fucking desperate for release that nothing else even matters anymore.

I see goddamn stars the second that I start to move my fingers, rubbing my clit in circles. My hips start grinding up, desperate for any ounce of friction, desperate for anything and everything all at the same time.

I start cumming, my mind not even catching up with my body as I groan out a moan, my body pulsing with need, pulsing with pleasure, my every cell in bliss. I haven't cum like this, not this hard, not this fast and desperately, from just a few small touches, from just a few circles of my fingers.

I hear him, right out of the edge of my consciousness, my ears barely fucking working as pleasure thrums through me, but I hear him groan, his orgasm ripping through him too, both of us falling off the edge together, and it crosses my mind that he was just as turned on as I was, just as desperate, just as needy, and he was just doing a better job of showing self-restraint, not showing me how fucking influenced he was.

I start to come down, my entire body feeling sore from clenching all of my muscles while I climaxed. I try to catch my breath, my breathing erratic as I suck in air, desperate for oxygen now that I've had my orgasm, now that I've felt that pleasure.

Reid is on the other end panting after his orgasm, seeming to come down in the same way I did, like the earth was shaken by how hard he just came. He breathes into the phone, and his fast breaths shouldn't be endearing to me, shouldn't make me smile as I breathe heavily, too. The sound of him on the other end shouldn't comfort me or make my insides feel a little gooey, but they do.

"Holy shit," he whispers, his voice hoarse, still breathing hard, unable to catch his breath, and I feel smugness radiate through me, happy to know that he enjoyed that just as much as I did.

"That good?" I ask, smug satisfaction taking over my voice, unable to hold back.

"Don't act like you don't know how good that was," he retorts, his voice soft, kind, humor radiating even through the phone. "I heard how hard you came. I would be shocked if no one in the hotel checks on you," he says with a smile in his voice, and I laugh, feeling closer to him than I have any right to.

I shouldn't be feeling this mushy feeling inside of me, but I am. I don't know why this is happening. I've had flings with people before, and I've had no problem walking away, but something about Reid, something about the way we trust each other, the give and take we have, feels different. I have never trusted someone like this, giving them every ounce of power that I can, and I've never had someone take such great pleasure in holding my power with kindness, making sure to take care of me in the process.

"Shut up," I finally reply, the silence feeling heavy between us as we both come down, our pleasure finally on the back burner, and now, as much as I don't want to admit it, I don't want to get off, don't want to end this here. I want to talk to him for hours, basking in what just happened between us, telling each other secrets like high schoolers, just enjoying each other. I shouldn't want this, shouldn't be itching for more when I already had the best orgasm of my life, but I am, and I'm not sure how to stop it.

Reid

"What was your first impression of me?" I ask. My voice is groggy with sleep, exhaustion finally starting to take over. We've been talking for a while, so long that I lost track of time. It's been nice being able to talk to her and get to know her without a time limit. We haven't been in a rush to get off the phone because we both had orgasms already.

"At the bar?" she asks before silence consumes the line. She is probably thinking, as her mind goes back to that night. I know mine does, the way she looked in that fucking dress, her head back laughing, and how she pulled every eye in the room toward her. She was radiant that night and, honestly, has been every night since.

"Or on the phone the first night," I murmur. I think back to that, to her guiding us, to her leading the phone sex because I was a little unsure, and it feels like such a contrast to where we are now, to this place we find ourselves. It feels like we are on the cusp of something. The pieces are starting to move, and that's scary but also so satisfying.

"At the bar, I thought you were hot, sexy, confident," she says lightly, a smile shining through her voice. "On the phone that first night, I thought you were endearing," she says, and I scoff, to which her laugh instantly echoes over the line.

"What does that mean?" I ask, smiling though. I hate how easy it is with her, how we can just talk about nothing at all, just go back and forth, and I'm having a good time no matter what. I've wanted a relationship for years. I've been waiting for someone to be a good match for me and to be the person who makes me want more with them. I have been waiting for too long... for her, and now, she's halfway across the country and hates the idea of even trying long distance. I think the universe is laughing at me right now.

"You were just so nervous, and I thought it was sweet," she says, and this conversation feels like it takes a turn. The entire world flips a switch, and we are suddenly serious, both of us feeling it, both of us knowing what is happening. I know she might not like this, talking about the real shit, the feelings that may be happening here, but I need to. I want to know exactly how she feels, exactly what she wants, exactly which way she wants this to go. It's all so confusing. I feel as though I am trying to go through this without having all the pieces to the puzzle. "I thought it was cute. You're so dominant, and I love that, trust me," she says eagerly, and it makes me smile. "But finding someone who can be vulnerable, try something new, even though you weren't perfect at it," she pauses, and I hold on to every word coming out of her mouth. I wouldn't interrupt her for the world. I am simply desperate for more. "I don't know, I just liked it." Her voice is timid like she gave too much away, but I'm itching for more, wanting to hear every thought she has ever had about me.

"It was only because I was with you," I admit, knowing I need to give something too, knowing that I want her to know at least how I feel. "You were so calm, so reassuring. You guided me through it, didn't make me feel stupid, just jumped right in, wanting to teach me, wanting to bring me along for the ride. I probably wouldn't have been so open with anyone else," I admit, my voice low, not knowing if this is the right thing to say, not knowing if I should even be saying this, admitting something so deep, but I want to, and that's the only thing I can use to guide me.

"I leave on Friday," she says, her voice so quiet that I almost don't hear her. I understand her meaning right away. This is supposed to end in just a few days. We are supposed to go back to strangers, people who don't know each other, especially not as intimately as we do.

"I know," I say, not knowing what else to say, not knowing how to make this better. Our reality is a fact. It isn't going to change. I don't know how to change this situation. Silence stretches on, neither of us speaking, neither of us breaking it. We sit in it, and for just a second, it feels like sadness, like we are both experiencing sadness together over this.

"If you lived closer, I don't think I would end this. I would just keep fucking you," she says, her voice sleepy yet serious, her words holding too much truth. I know she isn't lying, isn't just bullshitting me, and that only makes me sadder, makes the sting just a little bit worse.

"We don't have to stop talking on the phone," I say, my voice just barely hopeful, barely hinting that I want this. I want to keep doing this. I want to keep having the phone sex, of course, but I want this too. The late-night talks, the laughing, the deep conversations where we are both unsure if we should confide in each other.

"It isn't really the same," she says, and I feel my hope deflate. I return back to my feeling of not knowing how to fix this, not knowing how to change the situation we got ourselves into. We knew going into this that it would end, but I didn't expect us to grow closer as the days passed by. "I'm gonna go to bed. Talk tomorrow?" she asks, her voice a mumble, and I nod before remembering that she isn't here with me and can't see my movements or the expressions on my face. Maybe this would be easier if she could see me. Maybe if she could see every emotion as it crossed my face, if she could make them all out, she could decide for herself how I felt. No, how I feel. Maybe it would be easier if I could do the same with her.

"Yeah, talk to you tomorrow," I say softly, waiting for her to hang up the phone. My phone beeps, the sound that the call is over, and I set the phone on my bedside table, trying to shake it off. I am trying to get back to myself, to shake this feeling, this uneasiness, but I can't. I don't sleep well after that, my body stiff, unable to relax with Friday looming over me.

Chapter 12

Avery

My phone buzzes with a text on the lounger next to me, pressed against my skin. The sun shines bright against my eyes, and I bring my arm up to block it while I check my phone, trying like hell not to be too eager, afraid to tip off Emma that I'm hoping it is a certain person. She knows how to read me like a book, and I've kept my secret this far.

The text has a picture attached, a picture of Reid's boner through his pants, through his work pants, which is such a turn-on, thinking about him in a suit, in his office. Even more so, the idea that he is hard with other people around, trying to hide his desire for me while he's at work. I'm sure he's imagining all the ways he could fuck me in his office, with his suit still on, just his buckle undone and his zipper down, forcing me to be quiet so no one else hears us.

You make working very hard

I read his message, and I smile lightly, bringing my hand down from blocking the sun to reply. I type out my reply, not thinking too much, just wanting to enjoy this, the sun on my skin, my sister next to me, a hot guy texting me about his cock. Having my sister next to me is more awkward than anything, but whatever. I'm enjoying being surrounded by all these people I enjoy, feeling happiness for the first time in so fucking long.

Too bad I'm not there to take care of that for you. I would hide under your desk all day until you were satisfied.

I hit send, knowing it will drive him crazy, knowing it will only make his cock throb, but that's exactly what I want. He drove me crazy yesterday, keeping me right on the edge, keeping me from cumming. Still, as much as I enjoyed it and as hard as I came, I want to make him suffer just like he made me.

You are fucking evil, you know that?

I read his reply, shifting slightly to the side so my sister can't see who I'm messaging. I don't think she would care, don't think she would have a problem with it, but I also don't really want her to find out, not yet, at least, not if she doesn't have to.

I look down at my phone as it buzzes again

Imagining being in a client meeting with you under my desk... fuck it's driving me insane.

I bite my lip, trying to keep my reactions to myself, trying to be discreet, but I've always been shit at it, awful at hiding my emotions from anyone, much less my sister. I feel her eyes on me as I type out a reply.

I would see how deep I could take you while you talk to your client. See if your cock would hit the back of my throat, make me gag. I'd have to be quiet though.

I glance up at Emma, sitting in the lounger next to me, her eyebrows raised, a question in her eyes. I pretend I don't know what she is asking, sending her the exact same questioning look, our similarities definitely present.

"Don't play dumb with me," she says, her eyes squinting like she is trying to read text a little too far away. Her eyes search my face, giving me anxiety, and I feel my cheeks heat. I knew this was coming. I knew she would catch on before our vacation was over. I knew I couldn't keep it hidden from her, but part of me hoped to avoid this.

"I don't know what you're talking about," I finally reply, glancing away from her, not able to lie to her while looking her in the eyes.

"Who are you texting?" she asks, a knowing in her voice like she already knows it's a man. I glance at my lounger, picking at a loose thread, needing something to do with my hands. I don't like lying to her, don't like not telling her things. I'm not even worried she's going to be mad. She would probably be happy for me, probably excited that I found someone to orgasm with on a regular basis.

But this thing with Reid feels bigger than that no matter how much I tell myself it isn't, that it can't be. I'm not ready to tell her because this doesn't feel like a fling. It doesn't feel like a small blip in my history. This feels like a bigger deal, and I don't want to admit that to myself, much less her. I want to keep pretending that I feel nothing, that I'm not opening myself up in ways I never have before.

If I tell her, then I have to face it, and finally realize what is happening, and I don't think I'm ready to do that.

"You've been smiling at your phone for the past five minutes, and nothing makes you smile like *that*," she says, pointing to my face, and I wipe my smile off, completely forgetting it was even there, forgetting that I show every emotion right on my face.

"Like what?" I ask, doing my best to keep my voice soft and unbothered. I fail terribly.

"You are blushing," she says, her eyes glancing down at my chest, going wide, probably seeing how red it is, how my blush has spread not only to my cheeks, but to my chest. I don't look down. I don't want to know what my body looks like. Knowing what we were texting about, I'm sure I am blushing, and I am sure she can read it all over my face, but I hold strong, intent on getting her off my back until I want to talk about it.

"It's called a sunburn, Emma," I retort, turning my nose up at her.

"Ha. Good one. Your 'sunburn' wasn't there before you picked up your phone," she says, mocking my tone, adding air quotes and everything. I just roll my eyes, looking out to the pool, needing distraction. I let my body slump against my recliner, pouting.

"C'mon," she says, her voice soft, reassuring. "You can tell me anything." Her words make me feel guilty, make my secret feel bigger than it is, and I force the words to tumble from my mouth before I can second guess myself, before I can convince myself that this is a bad idea. I just push them, knowing it will come out eventually, knowing that since she is suspicious, I won't be able to keep this secret any longer.

"I'm texting Reid," I mumble, turning away from her, not wanting to see the look on her face when she processes exactly what I've just said.

"I'm sorry, what?" she asks, and I'm unsure if she is shocked or didn't hear me, so I turn toward her, my face warm with embarrassment, and say it again.

"I'm texting Reid," I say more clearly, and the way her eyebrows raise, the shock on her face, tells me she knows exactly what I said this time.

"Finn's best friend, Reid?" she asks, looking more confused than when she couldn't hear me.

"Yeah," I reply simply, anxiety spiking in my blood. I'm suddenly unsure how this is going to go. I was convinced that she wouldn't care, wouldn't give a shit, but now that I'm in front of her, I'm worried she is going to care a lot more than I expected.

"How do you even know him?" she asks, with no malice in her voice, just pure confusion, like we are two people she never thought would cross paths.

"The wedding, duh," I reply, giving my sister a blank look.

"Oh, right. I kind of forgot he was there," she says with a small wince and a laugh, looking at me like she has never seen me before, like sitting in front of her is a brand new sister, one she doesn't recognize. "Did you guys...?" she asks, her voice suggestive, a smirk taking over her gaze as she stares at me.

"No, we were going to. He was hitting on me at the bar, and I was about to ask if he wanted to join me upstairs, but he had a flight to catch," I explain, turning my body toward her, feeling relief that she isn't freaking out. I knew she would be okay with this, knew I could trust her with this information, and I'm suddenly happy that she knows. I needed someone to talk to, someone to bounce ideas off of because this whole situation has my head in a jumble.

"Were you going to fuck him in the middle of my wedding reception?" she asks, barking out a laugh along with her words. I feel my cheeks heat, again.

"Maybe," I reply, and she bursts out laughing. I follow suit, this entire thing feeling so ridiculous.

"Of course you were. I don't know why I'm shocked," she says, a look in her eyes full of adoration and love. I'm struck by how happy I am to be here, sitting with her in the sun, enjoying this vacation. I'm glad we stayed close, never letting anything come between us. "Anyway, so now you are texting? How did that happen?" she asks, turning her entire body toward me, crossing her legs on her chair, and I do the same.

"He gave me his number, but I wasn't even going to use it. I literally threw it in my purse, not even thinking about it, until I walked into my hotel room, and I was so drunk and horny. I wanted to hook up with someone, but no one was catching my eye, and I wished like hell that he was just here, so I picked up the number and called, and we had phone sex," I explain while Emma watches me closely, following along with the story.

"Oh my god," she shrieks. "Was it good?" she asks, her face filled with excitement, and I feel it leak into my expression, too, her joy contagious.

I think about the question for a minute, but I'm not sure how to explain what has happened between us these last few days.

"He had never had phone sex before, so there was a little bit of a learning curve, but it is pretty much just dirty talk, so he caught on really quick," I explain. Emma nods along as I talk, a smile on her face, like she knows something I don't.

"Oh my God, you like him, don't you?" she asks, her voice shrill, high, a shriek, and I wince at the sound.

"No!" I reply, too fast, already knowing she isn't going to believe me, isn't going to let me off the hook with that answer.

"Please," she says, her hand waving in front of her as if she doesn't believe me for a second, but that just makes me double down, forces this need inside of me to make her believe me, for her to understand exactly what is happening inside of my head.

"I don't. It's just phone sex. We are stopping after I get back home," I explain, looking out to the pool, trying to act casual, trying to act like it's not a big deal, trying to get my message across with my body.

"Be serious with me for a minute," Emma mutters, and when I look back at her, a glare in my eyes, she gives me a serious look right back, one that I tend to take seriously. I huff and move to face her, waiting for what I know she wants to say. "You would have told me sooner if it was *just* phone sex," she says, raising her eyebrows, challenging me to disagree with her.

I huff out another breath. This conversation is taking a turn I wasn't quite ready for. "I didn't know how you would feel about me having a thing for one of Finn's friends; that's why I didn't tell you," I explain, looking away again, not wanting to make eye contact as my stomach swirls with nerves.

"You are so full of shit. I have tried to hook you up with several of Finn's friends. No one would have cared. You didn't want to tell me because it isn't just sex. It's more than that, and that scares the fuck out of you," she says, hitting the nail directly on the head, taking my thoughts and my feelings directly out of my mind and spewing them back to me. I hate that her words feel right like my soul is exposed in front of me. I don't want her to be right. I don't want her to understand me better than I understand myself.

I sigh, wanting to deny it, wanting to pretend, wanting to put up a wall and act like she doesn't know what she's talking about, but this is Emma. This is my caring sister who knows when I'm lying. She knows me so well, knows when I'm full of shit, knows when I am annoyed. She will listen with grace and understanding and give me the best advice she has because she has never wanted anything other than good things for me.

If there is a person on this earth that I can trust with this, it's her.

"I didn't expect it to be so easy with him. I mean, it's phone sex, yes, but he's funny and sweet, and it's so easy to open up with him. I've never had this level of intimacy with anyone else," I reply, just saying it all, letting my thoughts and feelings pour out because this is my sister. She is the one person on this earth who knows all of my secrets, even before I do.

"And that scares you?" she asks, her eyes understanding, sincere. She waits as I think, trying to make my jumbled thoughts make sense.

"I don't want a relationship, you know that," I say simply, needing her to understand, needing her to know that this is not the time or the place I wanted this to happen. I don't want to settle down. I don't want to date anyone. Everything is just easier when it's sex, when it is hooking up with someone with no strings or feelings attached. I didn't want more when I started this, and I still don't want more. I don't want to push this thing between me and Reid to what it could be.

It feels easier to just cut the head off now, that is, to end this thing that is growing between us, but the longer that we talk and the more I see of him, the less I want to and that's the problem.

"He's a good guy, Avery. I've only met him a few times, but Finn talks highly of him. They have been friends for so fucking long, and he's the only one who didn't try to get something out of Finn when he got money. He seems to be a good guy, and I'm sure he would never try to hurt you on purpose," she explains, and her words stick in the air. It means something to me that the people in my life who I trust the most trusts him, but it doesn't erase my fear. It doesn't make the anxiety growing in my stomach calm.

"But I don't want anything more, Emma," I say lightly, the words falling from my mouth so easily like they have been said a hundred times.

"You don't want any more, or are you scared of anything more?" she asks simply, and then she pauses, letting her words get through my head, letting them sink into my skull and grow inside of my brain, taking up their own space. Then she sits up, her body rising in front of me. "I'm going to grab something to drink, try to find my husband, and make sure he hasn't spent all his money gambling. Just think about what I said, okay?" she asks, looking down at me, the sun shining behind her red hair.

I just nod, not wanting to speak, the air feeling too thick around me, her words seeming to weigh me down.

Everything she said catches in my head, leaving a trail of something behind, leaving a wonder, a thought that maybe she is right, that maybe I've just been scared, too worried to actually think about what could happen if I let this thing between Reid and I blossom.

I've never been one to operate on fear, never been one to want to let anything hold me back, and the idea that I'm letting it happen here, letting fear rule me, doesn't sit well with me. It scares me to think what could happen, how badly this could end, but it might scare me more to know that fear is holding me back, holding me from something that I really may want.

Chapter 13

Reid

I would love to be able to say that Avery hasn't been distracting me while I'm at work, that I'm such a professional that her texts don't keep me from doing my job, but fuck I would be lying if I said it isn't tough when I know she's sitting under the sun, in a tiny ass bikini, just waiting for me to get off.

Especially today, when her flirty texts are firing back, and I can't help but watch my phone for more and more and more, my body aching for release, desperate for her voice to be the one to get me to the other side of this lust.

I haven't replied to her in a few minutes, her message staring back at me, making me want to do dirty things, disgusting things, things I have no business even thinking about while I'm in my place of work.

I would see how deep I could take you while you talk to your client. See if your cock would hit the back of my throat, make me gag. I'd have to be quiet though.

I read it one more time, holding back a groan. I have my own office, and could do whatever I wanted, but it feels dirty with my co-workers on the other side of my office doors, with so many people around. I shouldn't want it as badly as I do. I shouldn't want to send her pictures and videos while I read her message over and over again and use the mental image to make myself cum all over my desk.

She is turning me into a fucking savage that doesn't know when to stop.

My phone vibrates on my desk, pulling me out of my thoughts, pulling me away from my lust, thankfully, but when I read the name, it all crashes back at me even harder than before.

I answer anyway, not caring about what I should be doing right now, just letting my body push me, letting all of my urges take over for once in my life because when it comes to her, when it comes to Avery, I can't seem to help myself.

"Hey," I say, trying to sound casual, trying to sound like her message didn't ruin me for the rest of my life, didn't make me second guess every choice I have made since the night we met. I try to hide the fact that I cannot stop wondering why the fuck I haven't called into work and found the next flight to her to finally get her out of my system.

The only problem is, I'm not sure if there is an "out of my system" anymore. I feel addicted. I'm like Pavlov's dog, getting hard anytime my phone rings, my body attuned to her and her phone calls. I'm a mess, and I only have her to blame.

"Did my message break your brain?" she asks with a laugh in her voice, the sound too sweet. I smile, leaning back in my chair, my cock literally aching in my dress pants.

"Maybe just a little," I admit, trying to keep my voice down. I've had hundreds of phone calls in here before, ones with clients whose information is top secret, ones where if someone heard, it could cost us millions, but none of them feel as important to keep secret as this one. I don't need any of the workers outside my doors to know exactly what is happening on the phone, or at least what I want to happen.

"I thought it might," she replies, her voice soft, sweet. I want to soak it up, lean into it. "Anyway, I'm just calling because..." she pauses, her voice suddenly unsure, and I sit up a little, not knowing what to expect. "I was just talking to Emma, and she got the information out of me," she admits, and I'm not really shocked by the news.

"She knows?" I ask, just wanting to be sure we are talking about the same thing.

"She knows," she says, almost grimly, like she doesn't know how I'm going to respond.

"Well, I guess I should be expecting a call from Finn anytime now," I say lightly, trying to add extra casualness to my voice, trying to convey that I don't care who knows that we are talking. It feels important to make sure that she knows that I'm not trying to hide this. I am not trying to shy her away from the world. I want her to know that I don't care if Finn is pissed or if Emma doesn't like it.

"Emma said something else," she mutters, the tone of the entire call suddenly changing, and I feel my heart start to beat, unsure what bad things Emma would even say about me. I have met her a few times, and every time, we got along. I thought she was kind, funny, and I assumed she felt the same. I hold my breath, waiting for her to continue.

"She said you are a really good guy," she says, and the statement shocks me; it's not at all what I was expecting. I wait for another moment, for her to explain, for her words to make sense, but they don't.

"That's what you wanted to tell me? That Emma thinks I'm a good guy?" I ask a small laugh in my voice, her meaning not coming through, not making any sense.

"And I..." she pauses again, this entire conversation confusing the absolute fuck out of me. "I missed you," she says, her voice light, fearful. I suck in a breath of air, hating how much her words hit me in the chest, making my entire body feel tense but in the best way. This moment feels big, the first time she is showing me that she cares, that she isn't here for sex, for a fling, and it seems important for me to respond the right way. I don't want to get too serious, to make this a confession for the both of us, make this a bigger moment than she already has, so I go with what we both know, what we are both comfortable with: sex.

"You are sitting by the pool, horny, aren't you?" I ask, trying to take the attention off her, trying to make this conversation light so that it doesn't scare her.

She pauses for just a moment. "You caught me. I'm just here, wishing your tongue was on me instead of my hands," she murmurs with a hint of relief coating her words. I smile, glad I got that right, glad she isn't running for the hills after confessing that she misses me.

"Are you touching yourself at the pool?" I ask, the image instantly consuming me, making it very hard to keep myself composed, even though I'm at work, the one place I should be pushing these thoughts away.

"Ugh, I wish, there are too many people here," she says, and I can imagine the way she is pouting just based on her voice, on the way she starts to mumble at the end of her sentence. "But I could always find my way to my room," she purrs, her voice like honey, and I want nothing more than what she is offering, nothing more than her moans filling my phone while I jerk off at my desk, but I know I shouldn't. I have so much work to do today, so many things are starting to pile up, and this thing between us distracts me and makes it harder and harder to get my work done. I need to be productive today, and I've already wasted enough time texting her dirty messages.

"I really should get some work done today," I mutter, not wanting my words to be the truth. I want to be there with her, on vacation, with all the time in the world to soak each other up, but instead, I'm here, in a suit, looking at financial reports, trying like hell not to let the numbers blur together.

"I actually need something from my room anyway," she says, and there's jostling on her side of the phone, like she is moving around, and I groan, imagining her walking up to her room in just a tiny little bikini, and me stripping it off of her with my teeth.

"I'm not kidding, Avery. I really do need to work today," I say, regretfully.

"Oh my God, calm down," she says with more jostling in the background. I don't have time today to play these games, even though my cock is already stiff in my slacks, and I want nothing more than to encourage her.

I hear the ding for the elevator, and I warn her, "Avery." I say it lightly, not knowing how I feel, not knowing which way I want to take this. My mind is warring, my rational winning out, just barely, the devil on my shoulder making a damn convincing argument, though.

"I just need to grab something from my room," she responds, a small smile in her voice, and I hold back another groan, not knowing what this woman is doing to me. I had morals and values before her, but where she is concerned, I throw them all out the window, not caring about them when she is around. I just need her. I need to be close to her, to talk to her, to hear her moans. Nothing else matters, and that's the exact wrong kind of thinking while I'm sitting at my desk.

"What do you need exactly from your room?" I ask, trying to call her bluff, trying to get her to admit to the game we both know she is playing.

"Lotion," she says after a small silence, and I don't believe her for a goddamn second.

"Really? Are you feeling dry right now?" I ask, a cheeky grin spreading over my goddamn face.

"Nope, pretty wet, actually," she replies, and I groan out loud this time, knowing exactly where this is going. I know exactly what her goal is, but I don't know if I should give in or not. I want to hold my ground and be productive at work, but I want nothing more than to sink into her, especially for the limited time we have. I'm not sure where this thing between us is going to go, and I want to savor it, want to soak it up so fully, until every moment is ingrained in my brain.

I hear the elevator ding again, and then a few seconds of silence, more jostling, and then there is a door closing, and I know she is inside of her room, and holding onto my self-control is about to get ten times harder.

"What are you doing?" I ask, going a little insane from the silence. I want to know exactly what her hands are doing: if she is touching herself, if she has taken off her bikini yet. I want to know, even though I know I shouldn't, even though I know this is a bad idea while I'm at work. I should be ending the call, hanging up the phone, but I can't help myself, can't seem to stop myself.

"Just laying in bed," she says, her voice a fucking tease. She knows exactly where she has me, knows exactly how on edge I am right now, and she's riding it out, making me more and more desperate.

"Avery," I warn again, my mind literally pulling me in two separate directions. I want one thing, but I know it's wrong, and I know it would be a bad idea. The walls of my office are too thin for this. It's a risk to even be on the phone with her, speaking to her like this while in the office. I can't jerk off, can't stroke my cock while she is talking to me, playing with her tight little cunt on the other end of the phone, not here.

"What?" she says, her voice a mock innocence, and I think of all the things we would be doing if she was here right now. I wouldn't be able to resist bending her over my desk, holding a hand over her mouth, and keeping her quiet while I fuck her senselessly. I wouldn't be able to say no then; as it is, I'm barely holding onto my self-control.

"I can't do this while I'm at the office," I warn, my voice barely commanding, barely holding any weight, because my self-control is slipping, and she hasn't even done anything. The silence is enough for me to want to cave, to want to break and just have my filthy way with myself, with her, even though she is too far away for either of us to be fully satisfied.

The distance between us just keeps feeling longer and longer the more we talk. It feels like a weight on my chest, and I just want to see her, want to see the women I've been talking to, been building a connection with.

She might not want to call it that and might be hesitant to admit what is happening, but that's what it is. We are building something, no matter how much we shouldn't, no matter how much it is setting both of us up to get hurt, to get fucked over. Falling for someone hundreds of miles away is never a good idea, but I don't think I can help myself anymore.

It's like a snowball rolling downhill. It's only getting bigger and bigger, collecting more as it goes, and there's no stopping it, no slowing its roll.

"I'm just laying in bed, Reid. I don't know what you think I'm doing," she says, a smile in her voice. It sounds so fucking sweet, and I groan because we both know where this is going, and I'm not strong enough for this.

"You are such a brat, you know that?" I ask, my voice hoarse, the anticipation making this worse, making my entire body thrumming. I just want her to be touching herself, to be teasing the fuck out of me already, but knowing that it's coming, knowing that she is going to soon, is ruining me.

"Yeah, I know," she murmurs with a smugness that shouldn't be sexy, but it is. "Did you think I was going to do something else? Something dirty?" she asks, and my entire body withholds a shudder. I don't know how she did this, how she got me so completely wrapped around her goddamn finger, but here I am, listening so intently to every word coming out of her pretty mouth.

"Avery, either play with your little pussy, or I'm going to hang up on you and make you wait," I say through clenched teeth, my resolve completely slipping now, my desire to listen to her, to hear her cum, is too overpowering. I don't have to do anything, don't have to jerk my aching cock, but I need to hear her cum, need to have her orgasm ringing through my ears if I'm going to get anything else done today.

"Fine, so demanding," she quips, acting like she isn't influenced by this, but I can hear the way her breathing has picked up, the smile in her voice, the desire there too. I can hear it all. I've become a master at listening for her subtle clues, the tiny hitches in her voice, and exactly what they mean, and right now, I know she wants this as badly as I do.

"Tell me everything that you're doing," I say, trying not to sound like I'm begging or like I'm pleading with her, even though we both know that if she denies me, I will. I'll ask very nicely if that is what she needs because this desire running through my blood is too hot and too all-consuming. I can't push it away, not anymore.

"I'm moving my bikini top to the side, exposing my tits," she says, her voice light, slow, like she is still edging me, and I fucking love this side of her. I've always been a dominant man, liking taking control in the bedroom, liking calling all of the shots, making women just listen to whatever I have to say, but having her tease me like this is ruining me for anyone else. "I'm bringing my hand down on my stomach, sliding it down, down, down," she purrs, and I swear to god I'm holding onto every word, my entire body tense as she describes this.

"You are going to pay for this," I mutter out, my mind thinking of a hundred ways that I could make her regret this entire tease, this entire situation. My head spins with all the ways I could make her beg for mercy, beg for her orgasms, instead of the other way around.

"Not today, I'm not," she says, like a true brat, like someone loving having all of the power, like someone who relishes in my misery. I need her so desperately, like I need air, and I suddenly want to ask for more than I'm allowed, more than she would be okay giving me. I want to fly to her and show up at her hotel room with nothing but a bag in my hand. I want to explore this, find out why I feel like this. I want to be surrounded by her constantly and find out if she feels the same way. I've been wanting this more and more, and it feels so intense inside of my chest, this desire to feel the heat of her skin against mine, to feel her lips against my own, to feel her body under me. It's harder to brush off now, now that we've had a few days of talking, of getting to know each other.

"Avery, I'm supposed to be working," I say, my voice barely able to hold any warning, but I hear people moving outside of my office. I can hear them talking through the sheetrock, but it only makes this hotter, only making my cock stiffer that someone could catch me.

"You don't have to do anything, Reid. I was just planning on making myself cum real quick, but if you don't want to listen, no problem," she says as if it means nothing, as if she barely wants me here, but we both know it's a lie. We both know this is a game we are playing. We both know that she loves this, drawing it out, making me ache for her. She loves knowing she has me right in the palm of her hand.

"Fuck," I curse, my cock literally throbbing through my slacks. "I want to hear it," I say, my voice so fucking low, like I don't want to admit to this, and I don't. I hate that she has me here, but part of me, the small part inside of me that I only seem to be able to show her, kind of loves it, kind of loves the way she can command the room, can command me, can put me in the palm of her hand. She has so much power, and I have no problem admitting that because she is a force, and we both know it. It only makes it that much sweeter when she gives me all of the control.

"I thought you might," she snides, her voice full of satisfaction, and I'm about to quip back, annoyed at her tone, but I listen as she moans, probably bringing her hand down on her clit and rubbing circles in her sensitive flesh.

Every thought I have ever had goes out the window, and my only concern becomes her pleasure, becomes her orgasm that is in the future. I want it, so desperately, to hear her come apart.

I rub my cock through my pants, needing some kind of friction, some kind of relief, but I don't stroke as much as I would like, as much as my body needs, because if I'm not careful, I'm going to cum in my pants like a fucking teenager, unable to handle a little bit of heavy petting.

"You going to be a good girl and cum for me? Make me listen to your orgasm and wish I was there? Feeling it on my cock?" I ask. My entire body is tense. I need to hear her. I need to hear every sound that comes out of her mouth. I need to know how much she is enjoying this and how much she needs this. I need her to want this as badly as I do because it is the one thing we agree on. I know I can't ask for more than this, can't ask for her to consider what we could be, but this, we can do this.

"Yes, fuck yes," she moans, her breath panting against her phone, and I revel in the sound, rubbing my cock to each breath she lets out, letting her pace guide me.

"Play with those big fucking tits too, baby. Show your body how good it can feel," I murmur, my orgasm already too close, already building at the base of my spine, and I want it, want to have phone sex with her in my office, no matter how inappropriate it is, no matter the goddamn consequences, but I rein myself in, needing to keep myself at least a little under control.

"Fuck, I'm so fucking wet for you," she mutters, her voice so sweet, so desperate, and I love that she slowly gives the power back whenever she gets closer to orgasm.

"That's right, baby, it's all for me," I say, and I hope it's okay to take possession of her pussy, of her wetness. I want it all. I want to be the source of everything good in her life. I could burst with this feeling, this desire, this need to be closer to her. It feels like an itch that I can't quite scratch, can't quite satisfy because I'm never there with her, never feeling her clench around my cock, never feeling her breath against my skin, her moans in my ear. I'm not experiencing everything she has to give me, but now I am starting to wonder if it would ever be enough, if I could get enough of her. The longer I talk to her, the hungrier I get for even an ounce of her attention. I just want more of her, more time, more conversation, more orgasms, and it feels like we are chasing the clock because I know this has a deadline.

"Yes, all for you," she agrees, and I know she's getting close. I imagine her playing with her tight cunt, her legs spread, her body on display, her desire radiating off of her as she gets closer and closer to cumming.

An idea suddenly pops into my head, payback for this tease that she has given me. It might be a good idea, or it might be awful, but I know I'm about to find out because I can't hold back, can't stop myself from saying exactly what I'm thinking.

"Are you close?" I ask, wanting to know for sure, needing to hear her say it.

"Fuck yes, I'm so close," she moans, her voice barely a breath.

"Good. Are you going to do exactly what I tell you?" I ask, wanting her to agree, knowing that the closer she is to her orgasm the more likely she is to do what I want.

"Yes, yes, anything," she says. Her voice is a cry, a plea, for me to make her finally cum.

"Stop," I say, the one single word seeming to take up all the space between us, and the line goes quiet just for a second before a whimper ghosts over my body, her whimper making me shiver.

"What?" she asks, but I know she was listening, because she is breathing heavily and slowly catching her breath. She is making these noises, whimpers, like she can't wait to touch herself again, like she is begging to touch herself again.

"Brats don't get to cum," I say, taking all of the power back, enjoying this give-and-take we have with each other, this desire for both of us to be in control. "Wait until I get home, and then I'll call and let you cum," I say, now my voice filled with smug satisfaction. Now I'm the one boasting, enjoying having this control over her.

"You don't get to control my orgasms!" she erupts, her voice a shriek, and I do my best to hide my chuckle, enjoying how crabby she gets when she is horny. Something to remember for later.

"I don't. You are your own person. You control your body, but I think you're going to listen to me," I say, maybe a little too surely. She could just disregard me, just give me the finger and make herself cum, but what is the fun in that. She knew a punishment was coming. She knew I would do my best to get back at her, but she didn't expect it right away, which is why this is perfect.

"You've got to be fucking kidding me," she says, her voice a low whisper, and it's that moment that I know she will listen. She will wait to cum until later when I call her back.

"Call you later," I say with a smile, then quickly add, "No cheating," I warn, and then I hang up, leaving her stunned without an orgasm. It isn't completely just her punishment though because my cock is still hard in my slacks, and I didn't even get to hear her orgasm to get me through the day, but I'm willing to suffer just to know that she is suffering even more, sitting on her bed, her cunt dripping on the goddamn sheets, begging to be touched.

Chapter 14

Avery

I stare at my phone, my home screen greeting me, my mouth hanging open. I cannot believe how that turned, how quickly I went from about to cum, on the cusp of orgasm, to literally being denied, to staring at my blank phone, having to wait until Reid gets off work to fucking cum.

I huff, the rebellious part of me wanting to push on, to make myself cum anyway, because why not? He wouldn't know. I wouldn't have to tell him, but that idea, the idea of going against him, just doesn't feel right. He's not asking me not to cum to actually make me suffer, but to make the anticipation rise, to make it that much better later. I know this, yet the idea of going back down to the pool and finishing the rest of my day does not appeal to me one bit. I don't want to walk around with an aching pussy, begging to be fucked. I want to walk around with a glow from a good orgasm.

I huff again, already knowing what I'm going to do, already knowing how the rest of this day is going to play out, but not wanting to admit to it. I want to hold on to the belief that I'm going to cum for just a second longer.

I right my bikini top, covering my tits, my nipples literally aching to be touched, begging for more, but I push on, getting out of bed and going to the bathroom, trying to get rid of some of my wetness because I know it's just going to distract me all day. As if it matters, as if anything will take my mind off the orgasm I was about to have.

I hate to admit it. I really fucking hate it, but this entire situation, him telling me not to cum, does make it a little more exciting, does make a thrill run up my spine. I can't wait for tonight, for the moment that my phone rings, his call being all the permission I need to finally give my body some goddamn relief.

My mind races thinking about tonight, about how it's going to go. If he's going to make me wait or tell me to make myself cum the second he picks up the phone. If he's going to cum too, or just listen to me, listen to me get off after waiting so long. It probably won't even take long, only a few minutes of playing with myself until I'm exploding, my entire body going rigid with release.

I feel my cheeks heat. I pass the mirror in the bathroom and glance at myself, looking at my rosy cheeks, but that's not the only thing I notice. I look good. I look happy, like I have some light back in my eyes. I stare at myself for just a second, basking in it, trying to piece together exactly what is different, exactly what has changed in the last week, but there's really only one thing, and I don't want to admit what, or who, it is just yet.

Chapter 15

Reid

The day goes by slow, too fucking slow, and the entire time I'm second-guessing myself. I don't know if she finds this as hot as I do, the idea that she is writhing, horny but can't do anything about it, begging for release. I like the idea of her being on edge all day, waiting for my phone call, waiting for me.

I just hope she feels the same, feeling the thrill of this. I hope she feels the desire shooting through me and how badly I want this. I've never had this with anyone else, this trust, this ability to do the things I desire, to act out some of my fantasies. With her, I barely second guess it in the moment though because I know if she doesn't want it, we would just talk about it. We have a phone between us, and that makes it so much easier.

It's not just that, though, is it? Just the phone? I don't think so. I think we just work in a way I never expected. I didn't think any of this would happen when I talked to her at the bar. I thought we would be a one-night thing, just what she expected, and now I'm sitting here, at my desk, counting the seconds until I can get off work to talk to her again, to make her cum, yes, but just to hear her voice too.

It isn't just the phone sex anymore, just the idea of going home and cumming with her on the phone. It's the before and the after. It's the talking and joking and the texting. It's all of it. This is so much more than I thought it was going to be, and although I'm okay with it, okay with the idea of this being more, I know she is hesitant and has been since the beginning.

But I can feel her start to break, start to show me that she is in this too, in these feelings. I just don't know what to do. I don't know what she needs to make this easier. It's so tricky to work all of this out when it's just ideas. We aren't in love, aren't each other's person. We just have an idea of something we could be, and that makes it harder to decide what moves I should make, especially when I know she is two seconds from walking away from this.

Finally, fucking finally, it hits five, and I am the first one out the door. Usually, I stay late, trying to get a little extra work done. I like to make the next morning a little easier but not tonight. Tonight, I want to be home as soon as possible. I cannot let this punishment be dragged out any longer because the longer I have to wait to call her, the more it feels like a punishment for me, not her.

Chapter 16

Avery

I lay on my bed, my breathing fucking ragged, as I come down from my orgasm, neither of us lasted long after waiting all day. The second he called, I was touching myself, not able to wait another second, and to my surprise, he was too, just as keyed up as I was, as if he was the one who didn't get to cum together, who got pulled right from the edge of an earth-shattering orgasm.

I'm tired from the orgasm, exhausted, really, but no part of me wants to get off the phone now that the phone sex is done. I'm trying to soak up every minute I can, my pride seems to take second place to my desire to be with him, surrounded by him.

My plane ride is tomorrow, ending my vacation, and I know I should be upset about that, about having to go home, but the part that I'm dreading, the part that makes my stomach roll, is the idea that I'm supposed to stop talking to Reid. I know we don't have to, that it's mostly my choice to end this little phone fling, but the idea of just continuing this, just talking to him, never getting the real thing, seems like torture. I don't want to put either of us through that, no matter how much I may want to, no matter how tempting it is. I feel like it will just hurt us more, make it more awful when it doesn't work out between us. I know I should just rip the bandaid off, but I have never wanted anything less.

"What are you thinking about over there?" Reid asks, his voice groggy. Both of us are exhausted after that, even though it is far too early to sleep yet. Maybe this whole situation is just draining for us. We have given this our all, given each other so fucking much, and now, tomorrow, we are just supposed to end it, just supposed to go back to our normal lives as if the other doesn't exist. It feels ridiculous, but I'm not sure what other choice we have.

"Just trying to plan for tomorrow," I mumble, not really wanting to say the words, not wanting to speak about tomorrow, about what is supposed to come. I just want to stay in this moment, with the both of us tired from orgasms, his sleepy voice greeting me, lulling me to sleep way too early, but we don't care because time doesn't seem to exist when we are on the phone. I want to stay right here, for the next ten years, giving myself a real chance to soak this up, to enjoy this. I want to freeze this moment and let both of us just enjoy each other's company without the stress of tomorrow.

"What time is your flight?" he asks, breaking my little happy bubble, my dream that this doesn't have to be the way it is.

"Twelve twenty," I say lightly, not wanting to talk about it.

"Are you excited to be home?" he asks, his voice light too, like neither of us know how to discuss this, like a dark cloud just came over both of us, taking our exhausted mood and making it sad, making it dull.

"Kind of," I say, my answer truthful. After this week, after all that we have shared, the truth seems to be the only thing I can give him.

"So... it's your last night then?" he asks, as if he doesn't want the answer, and if I'm honest, I don't want to give it. I didn't think about it before. I didn't want to, but he's right. This is my last night, the last night that I'll spend in this bed, and that means more than I want it, more than I want to even admit to myself.

"Yeah," I say softly, my voice not feeling strong, the lump in my throat feeling too big to talk around.

"And you don't want to keep talking when you're home?" he asks, his voice just a hint of hopefulness, just barely, and I swear it breaks me in two, makes all of my emotion flood out, and I suddenly don't want to talk about this, don't want to even go there because it feels like too much. It feels like I'm about to break now instead of tomorrow. This feels too much like a goodbye, and I don't want it to be. I don't want to say goodbye to him, to what we found together.

"I don't think it would be good to keep going. I'm already too..." I pause, not knowing if I want to admit this, not knowing if I want to give him every single thought inside of my head, but I move forward, knowing I need to say it all, to have no regrets. "Attached. I think it would just hurt me more if we kept talking, and we had no hope of ever actually seeing each other," I say, my voice a quiver, but I don't care.

I need him to know, to know that this wasn't just a week-long fling. I don't know what it was because it's only been a week. It's not long enough for things to blossom the way they could have, but that's the thing: they could. We have the potential to become something more. I guess that's what we are right now, just potential, but the distance has suffocated it, burnt out all the embers that could have made a fire.

"You're attached?" he asks, like he doesn't fully believe me, and I just stare for a second at the room around me, taking it all in, this whole moment.

"Of course I am," I admit, not knowing how he doesn't know, not understanding how my emotions aren't written all over these goddamn walls.

"Change your flight," he blurts out like he needs to rush the words or else he will hold them back. My eyes go wide, his words not seeming to make sense inside of my brain. "You have the rest of the weekend off work, right?" he asks, his voice a fucking plead, and it brings me out of my silence.

"Yes," I reply, my voice full of fear and uncertainty. I don't know what to do, my mind is a whirlwind as I go over every option, his words only making this more and more and more confusing.

"Come here instead. Change your flight to here, and then you can fly out on Sunday," he says, as if it is simple, as if it is easy.

"I can't just change my flight," I say, but I don't know why I couldn't. The most I would lose is money, but I have enough to pay for an extra flight. It would suck, but I could do it.

"There's a flight for here tomorrow at nine in the morning. I'll pay for your ticket right now, literally just say yes, and I'll buy it and send you the details," he says, his words jumbling together, my entire brain misfiring as I try to make a decision.

"Did you just look that up?" I ask, not knowing how he knew there would be a flight tomorrow, how he researched so quickly while my head is still spinning from the first sentence he said.

"I looked yesterday," he admits sheepishly, and I can imagine him scratching the back of his neck, avoiding eye contact, his cheeks pinking with embarrassment. "Look, I know this is insane, and I'm probably acting crazy, but I want you here in my bed. I want to figure out what the fuck is going on between us because we both know this wasn't a fling. But, the only way we can do that is if we actually try, and I want to try," he says, and his words feel so big, feel so scary, but part of me wants to jump, wants to figure out what the fuck this is, just like he said.

The other part, though, tells me that relationships are scary on their own. Relationships are hard, two people coming together, much less long distance. It's going to be too difficult, going to make me get my heart broken more than likely.

This part of me screams for me to just hang up, forget this thing with Reid ever even happened. Forget it all, push it out of memory, and go back to work like the scared person I am.

But I don't want to be like this anymore. I don't want to always be running away from stuff that could be amazing. I don't know what this is going to be. I don't know if I'm even going to like him when I meet him, but I know, at the very least, I want to figure it out.

"Okay, get me the ticket," I respond, even though my heart is racing and my stomach is in knots. I hear him click on his computer, sealing my fate, and although I'm fucking terrified, I know this is the right choice, no matter what happens.

The night goes quickly, both of us making plans, him sending me the info, me looking up the flight details, trying to figure out if I can get home by Monday, and when we get off the phone, none of my nerves are gone, only multiplied.

I get the worst sleep of my life, tossing and turning and wondering what the fuck is going to happen tomorrow, if this is even a good idea, to begin with, but right under all the worry, every scary emotion I have brewing inside of me is an excitement that I haven't felt for fucking years.

Chapter 17

Avery

This doesn't feel like me, doesn't feel like something I would normally do, and although it is making me feel like I'm going to throw up every second, honestly. I kind of like the mix-up from my normalcy. I'm sick of doing the same things over and over and over again, sick of being in the same spot.

I've been so against relationships, and I don't even have a reason for it. I don't have anything big in my life that has made me hate the idea of being with someone like that, but I do. I'm so scared to fully open myself up to another person. I just haven't wanted to do it, haven't wanted to get hurt, haven't wanted to put my trust in another person, but Reid, it feels different. It feels right to trust him with this, to ask him to take care of my trust. He feels like the kind of guy who can do that and can keep his promises.

All of this doesn't mean that I don't want a little reassurance though.

My new flight, the one that Reid sent me details for last night, leaves earlier than the flight I was on before. I wasn't supposed to leave the hotel until check out, at eleven, but instead, I'm up at seven, trying to catch this new flight with anxiety swimming in my gut. I have to go find Emma and tell her what is happening, to explain that I'm not going home, not immediately. And maybe, she will tell me that this is a good idea, that taking this chance will work out no matter what happens.

I pack up my room slowly, my anxiety taking up all of the space inside of my head, making me forget little things. I get fully packed, my bag zipped, before I remember that I have clothes in the drawers. I pack those too, and then remember to grab my phone charger, which is still sitting plugged into the wall next to my place on the bed.

I do this a few more times before just doing a big sweep, finding a bunch of miscellaneous stuff that I didn't have the brain power to think about. I feel like a mess, but I keep moving, doing my best to keep moving, to keep my body in a forward direction, because I know, the second that I stop, I won't get back up.

I close the door to my hotel room, sending a little goodbye to it inside of my head, sad to be leaving but happy with what I found there. I didn't expect it, didn't think this was going to happen to me, but I may be leaving with more than I came with.

I knock on my sister's hotel door in a rush, my fist communicating my frantic energy before I even have a chance to. She opens the door, her hair a mess, a smug smile on her face.

"I don't even want to know what you were doing in there," I say, not needing another visual of my brother-in-law, as if I don't already have enough.

"You *really* don't," she says in a gush. She glances down at my bag, a hint of confusion coming over her features. "I thought your flight wasn't until this afternoon?" she asks, her eyes darting back up to mine.

"I changed my flight," I say, desperate for her to understand, for her to know the meaning behind my words before I have a chance to say them, but she just looks more confused, more unsure of what the fuck is happening.

"Changed your flight? What are you talking about?" she asks, ushering me to the side, stepping out into the hall in nothing but her silk robe. I don't have time to comment about how cute she looks, how well and truly happy she has seemed since the wedding, because I'm too in my own head, too bent out of shape about what has happened within the last twelve hours.

"Reid asked me to come see him for the weekend, and I said yes," I say with a wince, not trusting that her reaction will be what I need, will be uplifting and give me the boost that causes me to get on the plane. I'm already worried I'm going to back out, that I'm going to wait in the airport and sit until it's time for my flight back home.

"Oh my god," my sister exclaims, looking happier than I expected. "Oh my *god*, I'm so excited for you!" she says, looking me up and down, her eyes lighting up.

"You don't think it's a bad idea?" I ask, my anxiety spiking even at the question, at the idea that this could potentially be a bad plan.

"No, I think you've been staring at your phone like a love-sick puppy for the last week. Go get your man," she says. When my eyes grow wide at her words, she assures me, "or just go get laid. It doesn't have to mean anything yet, but either way, you deserve this. Just go have fun," she says with a soft smile, coming closer to me, putting her hand on my arm, comforting me instantly.

I pull her in for a hug before she has a moment to back away from me. We aren't that touchy and feely, but I need this, need my sister to make this feel a little bit more doable.

"He's a good guy?" I ask, needing one last shove, one last reassurance that this isn't the worst idea of my entire life.

"He's a very good guy," she says, the smile never leaving her face, her excitement for me literally bouncing off the hotel walls. I step back, knowing I need to leave, knowing I need to catch my flight, but I hesitate, my feet not wanting to move.

"Call me when you land," Emma says, stepping back, waiting for me to move. I don't think I just act. I nod and start walking, forcing myself to take it just one step at a time, no matter how fucking scary this is, no matter how high my nerves are. I've wanted this all week, to see him, to have his body against mine, his voice in my ear. I want it all, and now I'm about to get it. This isn't the time to get cold feet; this is the time for action, for movement, and that's what I do. I move, even if it makes me feel like I'm going to throw up.

Chapter 18

Avery

I grab my bag, finally, from baggage claim, looking around for the man that I met just a week ago. I have only seen him once, but I know his voice like the back of my hand. If only I could have everyone speak for just a second so I could know exactly where he is.

I grab my bag and roll it with me, glancing around in every direction, desperately trying to find Reid. My flight was uneventful. I was nervous the whole time, too scared to sleep or relax, so the entire time, I sat there tense, waiting for the plane to land, and half hoping we would get lost and never return to the ground. Someone had asked if I was a nervous flyer, and I just agreed, it being easier than explaining what was actually happening to me.

I glance around, my head moving in every direction, probably looking like an idiot, a nervous, terrified idiot.

But then I see him, holding up a stupid fucking sign that says "the girl who calls me every night" instead of my name. It makes me smile, my anxiety easing instantly, a familiar feeling taking hold in my chest, as I remember that the man standing in front of me is the same man who I have been talking to the last few nights. This is why I came here, because the way this man makes me feel isn't like anything I have experienced before.

I want us to be something, something that I know I shouldn't want. I should be holding myself back, not allowing myself to feel these things, but I do. I feel it all, and I want him in more ways than I should.

I approach him slowly as if I could spook him, and that's exactly how I feel. I feel like I'm going to push him away with these big feelings, but I don't know where else to store them other than right on my sleeve, right for him to look at, to inspect, to compare to his own feelings.

"Hey," I mutter as I walk up to him, his dark hair a bit of a mess, like he's been running his hands through it. His eyes are bright, a slight nervousness in them, but the same rich brown from the wedding. I'm half expecting him to hug me, to touch me, but he doesn't. He looks ahead, barely making any eye contact with me. I feel the nervousness in my stomach start to flutter, unsure of what he is doing. He's literally holding a sign that could only be addressed to me, and I remember what he looks like almost too well.

"Sorry, I'm waiting for this gorgeous girl," he mutters, sending me a wink as he talks. I start to understand, a smirk playing on my lips, my nerves still present. I barely keep myself from freaking out, this entire situation is completely out of my pay-grade. "We've been talking all week, and I think I have a little bit of a crush on her, but I'm not sure exactly how she feels," he mutters, looking away from me, not making eye contact, and I feel my face heat, my nerves fluttering in my stomach. "She's got a filthy mouth on her, too. Drives me fucking wild," he says with a smirk, finally looking at me, finally making eye contact with me, and his gaze sweeps me up and down, consuming me.

I dressed for this moment specifically, wearing tight leggings and a tight long sleeve, for him to check me out like his life depends on it, and he does. He looks me over like he wants to eat me alive, like he could devour me right here and now if I gave him the chance. He looks at me like I hold all of the power in this dynamic, which couldn't be further from the truth.

"She must be really hot if she has you waiting out here for so long," I murmur, his eyes still trailing my body, my skin starting to tingle under his gaze, excited to have his eyes on me for the first time in months.

"God, she is," he says, continuing to devour me with his eyes. "I was thinking of asking her to dinner, but I don't know if it's too much," he mutters, his eyes finally connecting with mine again, vulnerability showing, and my stomach lurches, my ears ringing as I try to process his words.

"You want to take her to dinner?" I mutter, not sure I'm completely understanding. "Like a date?" I ask hesitantly, my eyes bouncing around his face, desperate for a clue on what he means. I feel my nerves flutter, but this time, with hopelessness, with school girl crush kind of feelings.

"Yeah, like a date. She's been hesitant to come and see me, but then she agreed to change her flight, and I can't help but wonder what that means. I just don't want to read too much into our... situation." he says, his eyes bouncing down to my body again, hunger taking over, just for a second, before his eyes connect with mine again.

"What's your situation?" I ask, my voice small, my breathing coming out ragged. I hoped he wanted me. I have been desperate for a moment like this for a little while, but I didn't expect it to happen at all, much less the second I stepped off the plane.

"We help each other out," he says with a suggestive look on his face, his meaning known instantly. I feel my cheeks redden, thinking of all of the conversations we've had over the last few months, all of the nasty things he has told me he wants to do to me.

"And now you want to take her on a date?" I ask, my voice stronger, my confidence coming back, even just barely.

"Yes, but I don't want to freak her out," he says, hesitating before speaking again. "I like her, more than I probably should, and I don't want it to get weird if she doesn't feel the same," he mutters, his voice going soft, his vulnerability taking over, and my stomach flutters as I watch him confess his feelings for me.

I take a deep breath, feeling as if I'm dreaming, as if this couldn't have worked out as well as it is. This feels like something I imagined, like it can't actually be happening, but it is. He is standing in front of me, confessing that he feels the same way I do, and now the ball is in my court. I thought I would be waiting for him to make a move for an embarrassing amount of time, but it was like he couldn't hold himself back, like he needed to say it before he burst, and that only makes me like him even more.

"I'm sure that she would say yes to dinner," I say, biting my lip instantly, my heart beating in my ears, drowning out the background noise of the airport.

"For a date? Not just as friends who make each other cum over the phone?" he asks, hope lighting up his eyes, a small smile taking over his face. I smile back, not able to stop myself.

"Yes, as a date. I'm sure she feels the same way," I say, holding eye contact, trying to make him understand, trying to make him see how badly I wanted this moment to happen, but I wasn't sure if he felt the same, wasn't sure if jumping off the deep end was going to get me killed or get me saved.

"Thank fucking God," he mutters, his body moving instantly, the sign in his hands floating to the ground as he lets it go, darting over to me, his hands on the side of my face before I have a second to even process it. His lips are within an inch of mine, but he doesn't close the gap. He just stares at me as we share breath, both of us panting like we just made out for twenty minutes. "I have wanted to do this for a week," he mutters before his lips connect with mine, fucking finally.

Epilogue

Reid

The knock on the door catches my attention, and I make sure my tie is in place before speaking, a nervous energy running through me.

"Come on in," I shout out, keeping my attention on the door, on the meeting I'm supposed to be having right now, not on the woman sitting under my desk with my cock in her hand and a devilish smile on her face.

I don't even have to look down to know her smile, to know exactly how she looks, the smug smile on her face. She has always been a little siren, always loved the idea of keeping me on my toes, of keeping me in the palm of her hand, literally. I might hate it if she didn't let me do the same to her, control her body, her orgasms, whenever I want, trusting me with all of the control.

Avery flew in last night, just for today, Friday, and the weekend. We don't see each other as much as we should, as much as we would both like, but it doesn't matter. We just enjoy each other's company. We enjoy being around each other when we can, and we miss the hell out of each other when we can't.

We make up for it too, over the phone, in person, doing all of the nasty sexual things you can think of, desperate to soak each other up as much as we possibly can. Although now it isn't with an end in mind. We've been going steady for a few months now, and I don't see that changing. I don't see either of us getting sick of this or not finding it worth it.

That was my worry in the beginning. Relationships are hard—long distance ones even more so. We were set to fail or grow apart, but I think something about the way we found each other, that we started this whole thing over the phone, made it a little easier. We already knew what was going to come if we decided to try a relationship. We knew the struggles. We knew how hard it would be to only be able to talk on the phone. We knew, and we still decided we should try.

"Hey Reid, what's up?" John asks, poking his head into the room. I wave him over, motioning to the seat in front of my desk. I ignore the presence by my legs, the heat coming from Avery.

She is kneeling under my desk, out of eyesight, with my hard cock in her hand, doing these little fucking strokes that she knows I goddamn love. She is the devil, I swear to God. She always knows exactly what I need, always teasing me in a way that is the most perfect torture, and as punishment, I do the same fucking thing to her, loving every minute of it.

"I just wanted to talk about the expense reports for a moment with you," I say, keeping my voice steady, doing my best not to show that I'm currently getting jerked off under the desk by my girlfriend, trying to make sure he doesn't know.

I could get in so much fucking trouble for this, probably fired, but when Avery brought it up and asked if that was something we could do, I couldn't say no. I couldn't tell her it was too risky. She looked up at me with those fucking puppy dog eyes, and I was putty in her goddamn hands, yet again.

"Oh, sure. Does everything look okay?" John asks, sitting down, putting his elbows on his knees, looking up at me with concern in his brow.

I bring the sheet closer to him, showing him the line that doesn't look right, that throws off all of my other forms, and he nods, taking it from me and looking at it a little closer.

"If that is correct, then the rest of my forms are messed up, and then we need to go back and redo them," I say, still keeping my voice steady, doing my fucking best, but she is still jerking me off, going so fucking slow, too fucking slow.

We have been together long enough now, and I feel like I know her, know all the ways she acts, all the things that drive her wild, and I'm shocked she isn't trying to throw me off my game. She is being surprisingly nice, letting me keep my bearings, only giving me small strokes, only teasing me, something she usually doesn't do.

Of course, the second I think this, the second the thought crosses my mind, she puts her mouth on the tip of my cock, and sucks, giving the head of my cock all of the suction it needs, and I feel pleasure wrap around me, taking me hostage.

I hold back a groan, needing to keep my face neutral, but she starts rubbing her tongue on the underside of the head, pulling out every stop, trying to fucking ruin me. I push one of my nails into the meat of my palm, needing something to distract me, needing something to stop the pleasure from coursing through me.

She knows me too fucking well, and if she isn't careful, she is going to make me cum. Actually, if I had to guess, that's her goal, to make me cum while one of my workers is in the fucking room, to make me cum and try my best not to get caught, not to get fucking fired. She is playing a dangerous game, and I shouldn't find it this hot. It shouldn't be turning me on more, but it is.

The idea of having to hold myself back and keep myself from cumming while having a conversation, no one even knowing what is going on other than me and Avery, makes this entire situation so much fucking hotter.

"Do you think this could be a mistake?" John asks, looking up at me, confusion written all over his face. Avery licks the tip of my cock, swirling her tongue around it, and it is so fucking hard to keep still, to keep from making a sound, because she is fucking ruining me under there, giving me the best head I've ever gotten, and of course, I gotta keep quiet.

"I looked into it and found the receipt, but maybe we should ask Anthony first and see what he has to say. It may still be a mistake," I say, keeping my voice steady, barely a waver.

"Yeah, that's a good idea. I'll bring this to him. Can I have a copy of the receipt?" he asks, and then Avery takes my cock to the back of her fucking throat, holding back a gag, just fucking barely. We both know the sound would be too much and would give us away.

I reach down, opening one of my drawers, finding him the copy of the receipt, and then I place my hand on Avery's head, holding her down, forcing her to take my cock deeper. She is testing me, forcing me to take this pleasure, forcing me to keep a straight face, to keep from groaning, and if she is going to be like that, I'm going to steal the air from her lungs, making her take my cock as deep as she can.

I let go after a few seconds, giving her air, not wanting to push her too hard, wanting to take care of her still, and she pops off of my cock, probably breathing hard. I feel my dick twitch at the thought of her chest moving with her breaths, her big tits moving as she pulls in air.

God, I need John to leave right fucking now. I don't know how much longer I can take of this, of keeping quiet, of doing my best not to make a fucking sound, not to make an expression. It's about ten times harder than I thought it was going to be, and when it comes to Avery, I am not fucking strong enough for this.

I hand him the receipt, silently begging him to be on his way. This was exciting before, but I didn't realize how badly I would want it to be over...how badly I would need John to get the fuck out of my office so I could find some goddamn relief.

He lifts himself from the chair, looking over the piece of paper I just handed him, and for a second, I think I'm going to get lucky, think he is going to leave without even looking back at me, but instead, he turns around, looking me in the eyes just as Avery starts up again, swirling her fucking tongue around the head of my cock, my hips jerking under my desk. I do my best not to show a single emotion, even though I am itching to be down her throat again, itching to be inside of her, one way or another.

"Is Avery coming down this weekend?" he asks, our relationship being known across the office. We got mixed messages when I started to tell people I was seeing someone. Some of the older folks, who have worked here since they were my age, told me that it wouldn't work. Long distance never did, and I would be better off settling for someone here, like their granddaughter, perhaps. But, the rest of the staff was cool and gave me their best wishes.

My boss was the one who stood out, though. Because of this news, which seemed to somehow be the top of the office gossip for fucking weeks, I knew I had to talk to my boss about working my schedule out a little bit. I knew I would be asking for more time off for long weekends, and I wanted him to know why. I wanted him to understand that I'm just trying to see the woman who stole my goddamn heart, and he said he understood, said he met his wife when he was on vacation and couldn't get her out of his head. He said he would respect whatever I need, but if my work starts to go downhill, he will have no issue calling me out on it.

I, of course, was thrilled with that response, with the idea that this isn't all in our heads, isn't some fantasy we are playing out. I mean, I already knew that. I know that every second I look into Avery's eyes, or get a text from her, my heart races, but it is nice to have that affirmation, to have someone else's success story to reassure me.

"Yeah, she's c-coming down this weekend," I say, slipping for the first time, my voice wavering as Avery takes my cock to the back of her throat, fucking ruining me with that movement. Her mouth feels good, too fucking good. I'm becoming more and more addicted to her, wanting her constantly, pissed anytime she has to leave, anytime I have to leave.

Long distance works for us, we fight to make it work because what we have is just too good, but most days, I fucking hate it, hate being away from her, hate having to say goodbye, hate having to go weeks on end without sliding into her tight pussy, watching her tits bounce in front of me while she rides my cock.

"My wife wants to meet her. We should get drinks or something," he says, shrugging like it wasn't his idea, and I smile lightly, trying my best not to clench my teeth, even though every muscle in my body is tensing at once right now. I'm close, too fucking close, and Avery knows it.

She can sense it in my body, and I know she wants me to cum, wants me to fill her mouth full of my load, but I hold strong, trying like fucking hell to keep myself from falling off of that edge.

"Yeah, text me about it. We can figure out plans," I say, motioning to the door, probably rudely, but I don't care. I need him gone. Right. Now. "Close the door on your way out, yeah?" I ask, adding a smile, giving him a nod of appreciation, anything for him to take this the right way and just leave my office before I cum in front of him.

"You got it," he says with an easy smile, and he walks out, the door closing shut behind him, clicking into place.

I wait, one, two, three, before sliding my chair back, looking down at Avery with a 'seriously?' look, and she just giggles, the sound moving through my office, and it shouldn't turn me on more, shouldn't make my wet cock twitch, but it does. Everything she does seems to make my cock react.

She licks her lips, still under my desk, waiting for my command, waiting for me to tell her what to do next, and I love the power. I love the way she gives it to me, how she wants to please me. Part of me wishes she would misbehave by doing something that I don't like, just so I could bend her over my desk, slap her ass until it is fucking red, claiming her in the best way possible, but I hold back, knowing we both need relief right now.

"Bend over the desk," I say, needing her right now and not wanting to waste any more time. I can't take it, having her this close to me, not being inside her. This is what she has done to me, made me a fucking animal.

She obliges instantly, rising from her knees, bending over my desk, putting her ass on display for me. She is still fully clothed, which is a goddamn shame, so I walk slowly toward her, needing to feel her skin against my own.

I rub her ass, teasing her, needing her to be as on edge as I am, needing her to be right there with me. I feel crazy with this lust, insane actually, and I want her to feel it too, want her to be right on the cusp of completely breaking apart, just for me.

She whines in the back of her throat, moving her ass against my hand, begging for more, and I listen, not wanting to play games when this is what we both want and when we are both so fucking needy for this.

I pull her leggings down, leaving them by her ankles, looking at her ass in her black thong, loving the way it covers only the most intimate parts of her. I push down on her back, needing her to bend more, needing more of a view, needing more and more and more.

I pull her thong down, wanting her to be exposed, needing to see her pussy, and the second it is gone, she starts to fidget, her body knowing what is coming, her pussy knowing that my cock is going to be inside of her soon, and her body is begging me, so desperate.

I stare down at her, just for a second, getting my fill, needing to see every inch. I don't have the time to take this slow, to make her beg, and even if I wanted to, I need her to stay quiet, need her to keep ahold of herself just enough to keep from screaming out. I'm still not trying to get fired, no matter how much I keep pushing.

"Look at your cunt glistening for me," I murmur, watching the light shine on her pussy as she practically drips onto my desk, her desire so obvious. "This all just from sucking my cock?" I ask, already knowing the answer but wanting to hear it from her mouth, wanting her to talk dirty to me.

I think she conditioned me this way, made me desperate for her voice, always yearning for it. I think since we started over the phone, with only our voices to guide us, to show each other emotions, now I crave it, constantly.

"You…" she starts, stopping, probably biting her lip, just like she always does when she hesitates, and I wait, so fucking patient, giving her the time. I'll always give her the time, give her a moment to find her courage, because I can't stomach the idea of not hearing the rest of her sentence. "You pushed my head down," she says lightly, her voice soft, like she isn't sure of her words, and I'm blown back to when we started talking on the phone, her uncertainty, her fear, and I'm suddenly aware how much more confident she has gotten in us, how much more comfortable with me she is now.

"You liked that?" I ask, curious, my cock literally aching to do it again, to push her head down until she is struggling for air, begging me to let go, until she is choking on my cum and gasping for breath.

"God, yes," she says, backing her ass up, just enough for her to make contact with my cock, just enough for the heat of both of our bodies to meld together, and I groan, loving the way her skin feels against mine, loving having her close to me.

I slide the tip of my cock through her pussy, needing to move this along, needing more, needing everything she is willing to give me. She wines again, so needy, so desperate, so fucking vocal. I adore it, love every sound that comes out of her mouth, and so I do it again, just sliding my cock up and down, teasing her tight fucking hole, and she whimpers again, making my balls tighten instantly, my orgasm already too fucking close.

I give in, finally, not able to last another moment, and slowly slide my cock inside of her, so fucking slowly, making her feel every inch, making her feel every second of it. I watch as her head falls forward onto the desk, her body tensing under the pleasure, and I bask in it, loving the way I can influence her, loving the way I can see her pleasure just based on her movements.

"God, you're fucking soaked," I say, feeling how wet she is. My cock slides in so easily, and I fuck her, slamming into her tight cunt, desperate for us both to cum. "You gotta be quiet, okay?" I ask while slamming my cock into her again, grinding against her just the way she loves. I bring my hand down under her, bringing my fingers to her clit, rubbing small circles.

She whimpers, bringing her arm in front of her face, covering herself, trying her best to stay quiet while I work her body just how I know she likes. I take everything I know, and I use it all, doing exactly what she was doing to me just minutes ago. I want her to struggle to keep quiet. I want her to hold back a scream.

Half of the fun of this is that we could get caught and that someone could hear us. Someone could hear me sliding into her, hear our skin slapping together as I fuck her endlessly, could hear her little whimpers as she begs for more, and as she whines for me to make her cum.

She is breathing heavy and using all of her focus on not being loud, on keeping her noises to herself, and I fucking love it. I knew it from the first moment I had her moaning on the phone. I was an addict to her moans, an addict to the sounds she makes, and now I'm just constantly chasing them, wanting more, needing more.

"You gotta stop. I'm gonna cum," she says, wiggling around, trying to get me to move my hand, trying to get me to let her off easy. She wants me to stop because she doesn't think she can hold back and stay quiet, but I don't care. If I don't feel her cum on my cock, I'm going to die, going to combust right here. I need her orgasm. I need it more than I need to breathe.

"Then you're going to need to be quiet, huh?" I ask, a mock tone of voice. I love the way she tries to wiggle out of my grasp. A whimper escapes her lips while she tries. She is doing her best not to cum, trying like hell to get away from this, but I refuse to let her. Not after what happened under my desk. She tried so hard to make me cum with my co-worker right in front of me.

"No, I can't," she groans a little too loudly. I place my free hand over her mouth, keeping her quiet. I feel her bite into the palm of my hand, and I circle her clit harder, faster, needing to feel her clench around my cock, and she does, her orgasm hitting her full force.

Her legs start shaking, her body twitching against me, wanting more and less friction at the same time, and I can't help myself, can't stop myself from cumming inside of her, from orgasming right there with her, falling over the edge while she is clenching around my cock fucking squeezing me.

I slow my circles of her clit, trying not to overstimulate her, and we both do our best to catch our breath after our orgasms. She slumps against the desk when I let her mouth go, making a fucking mess of the paper sitting there underneath her, but I'll deal with that later. I don't care, not when she is here, in my office, in front of me.

I pull out of her, my cock sticky with my cum, and grab a tissue, cleaning myself up. I tuck my cock away and sit back on my chair. I pull her pants up, not bothering to clean her, to wipe my cum from her pussy, loving the idea of it dripping down into her underwear, of her walking around with my seed just sitting there all day, keeping her soaking wet.

I bring her back against me, my hand against her torso, and set her in my lap, letting her curl against me. She sighs, her back against my front, and I just hug her, enjoying her being here. I don't want her to leave again. I don't want her to go back home. I want her here with me, constantly. Long distance isn't a deal breaker, but it has made me a desperate man who can't ever seem to get enough.

"When is your flight?" I ask, not knowing if I want the answer. She always has to leave so quickly, never staying for more than a few days, never giving me enough time. I do the same thing, though. Both of us are so busy, our work calling for us. I want time to stop, for us to just have unlimited amounts of time together before it starts again. I want to sit in this bubble and pretend that the rest of the world doesn't exist.

"Sunday," she replies, and I groan, earning a giggle from her. The weekend doesn't feel like enough time with her. It never does, but I know, one of these days, we are going to figure something out, going to find a way to make this work, and going to move our relationship forward. We love each other too much for it to be any other way.

"In that case, give me an hour, and I'll leave early," I murmur against her back, feeling the heat of her against me, enjoying every second of it.

"Okay," she says happily, and I know I should get to work, that the sooner I let her go, the sooner I give her space to get comfortable on the couch in my office, the faster we can get out of here and go home, and I can take her to bed, but I just need another moment, need to feel her against me for just a little while longer.

"I talked to my job the other day," she says, her voice low, just barely nervous. I feel my curiosity piqued, and I hold her a little tighter.

"Hm?" I ask, wanting more but not wanting to push too hard, wanting to give her the time and space to get it out.

"They have a location here in the city and they said they would be open to a transfer," she says, a whisper, her voice barely making its way to my ears, but the second it does, my spine straightens, my entire body ridged, as I turn to her, needing to look in her eyes, to see if she is serious.

"Are you fucking with me?" I ask, my voice so serious. I need to know, need to know if I could actually have her here, have her in the city more often, have her under my roof, living with me, like I've always dreamed of.

"No. It would be a while before a job would open up here, and I would still probably be going back and forth between locations, but I could at least spend more of my time here," she says with a half-smile, her expression guarded, like she doesn't know how I'm going to respond.

I don't say anything, just crush her body against mine, sighing with relief, so fucking happy, so fucking excited.

"God, I fucking love you," I say, and she giggles against me, the vibration of her chest moving through my body too. I keep her close, not wanting her to pull away. I glance down at her, keeping out bodies tight together, and kiss her, savoring the taste of her mouth, for just a moment, my heart too fucking happy. I'm worried it is going to burst. I don't want to pull away but after a few moments, I do, staring into her eyes again.

"You're okay with this?" she asks, going back to uncertainty. I stare at her, fucking amazed, so blessed beyond belief, in awe of the fact that this woman, who has stolen my heart, is going to be here, even just part-time.

"I have literally never been happier," I say, the biggest fucking grin on my face, my entire body vibrating with happiness. She crushes her body against me again, both of us just sitting there for a few moments, content.

"I love you too," she whispers against my ear, and I'm so fucking grateful for her. I am grateful that she used my number that night, that she tried. I know how scared she was of a relationship, but she gave me a chance to show her exactly what we could be, and now here we are, moving forward together, exactly how I want it to be.

Books By This Author

Done Right (She Teaches Him #1):

What happens when Emma, who just wants to be done right, meets Finn, who doesn't know what he's doing?

Taught Right (She Teaches Him #2):

What happens when Joey, who just wants to be taught right, hires Ava, who knows exactly how to teach him?

F*cked Right (She Teaches Him #3):

What happens when Jace, who has never done this before, gets f*cked right by Callie, who knows exactly what she's doing?

Greedy:

What happens when the best kind of revenge, is fucking your ex-boyfriend's business rival?

White Christmas:

Their parents may be best friends, but Autumn and Theo have been enemies since birth. So what happens when they get snowed in at a hotel... and there's only one bed?

About This Author

Rhianna Burwell is an Amazon best seller in erotica. Author of the Before series and the She Teaches Him series, available on Kindle Unlimited, she takes pride in writing spicy, realistic, and deeply satisfying romance and erotica. Rhianna currently resides in Minnesota, where—when she's not writing erotica hot enough to melt all the winter snows—she enjoys curling up with her cat, avidly watching Grey's Anatomy, and reading—her current fav is alien romance. Rhianna loves to hear from readers, who can connect with via any of her social media links.

Instagram: @rhiannaburwellauthor
Tiktok: @rhiannaburwellauthor